# Feeling the Distance

## Robert John Goddard

# ACKNOWLEDGMENTS

Having an idea for a novel and turning it into a cover
picture design is hard. I want to thank Andrea for
creating a wonderful cover for *Feeling the Distance.*

andrea.price.concept

# 1

Although I am cold, I believe it is fear that is making me shiver. When night fell, I thought it was fear of the dark. Perhaps, this is a natural occurrence and the result of a survival instinct from our primitive ancestors when the night could conceal dangerous creatures. Closing my eyes brings comfort by giving me the illusion that I can control the darkness. But even with my eyes shut, there is fear of a hidden danger, of something I will not see emerging from the dead of night. And yet, if this time is part of the 24-hour period which dies and which ceases to move, I am not in the dead of night. I cannot see the man, but I can hear him breathing. It is soft and regular, but a whistle suggests there is resistance in the airways.

Josie is restless in her sleep. She occasionally makes speech sounds that drift away before they form meaningful utterances. Since the funeral, I have got to know her well. She is a mass of apparent contradictions. She can be impatient and persistent, belligerent and insecure, brave and cowardly. One moment she is in your face. The next moment she displays extraordinary sensitivity. I love her for what she is. Over the last 4 months, she has been my very own bright star on our journey of discovery.

This journey is almost over, but even after we left the hotel yesterday to climb this mountain, we never predicted that everything would come to an end in this bland mountain hut.

*

When Josie and I set off, there were only the two of us to breathe the freshness of early morning and to enjoy its suggestion of rebirth. The roofs of the houses were bathed in sunshine, and the upper walls were splashed with the red of geraniums growing from window boxes. After a few paces, the world changed. We entered the square and faced the dregs of the previous evening's demonstration.

The fury of that event had diluted to drifting shouts, knots of whispering people and the representatives of law and order circling the square with their hands on their truncheons. I was not anticipating a resurgence of violence, but I was anxious about the climb. Our training shoes and weather gear, although suitable for some English hills, were inadequate for the snow that lay in the *Oberwald* mountains. It was clearly visible, resisting the summer sun and holding out in the crags of the northern slopes. A glance at the weather vane intensified my unease. Swinging in doubt on the roof of the old school, the weather vane reminded me of the hotel manager's warning. The mountains above *Oberwald*, he said, were prone to sudden and violent storms. I swung my arms and whistled a favourite tune but as we set off across *Oberwald's* main square, my whistling sounded as flat as my mood.

We were passing the fountain when urgent footsteps

reminded me of the violent demonstration and alerted me to the possible danger of strangers coming from behind. I spun round and squinted at a man in military uniform approaching us in the sunlight. Telling myself that soldiers do not usually beat people over the head and take their money, I grabbed at Josie's elbow as an indication that we should be moving on. When the military man placed his hand on his truncheon, I hesitated. When he yelled, "halt," I froze.

"Your rucksacks," he said.

The peak of his cap threw the upper half of the soldier's face into a light shadow but I recognised him as the jester I had spoken to during the build-up to the demonstration. His eyelids flickered while he swore at our presence. When he stumbled on the cobblestones, he roundly cursed the stones, the street and the surrounding mountains. Unshaven and drawn, he raised his head and blinked at us over the bridge of his nose. Pointing at my rucksack, he signalled to me that I should remove it.

"And open it," he said.

I did as I was told. He crouched and stared into my eyes while he plunged his hand into the neck of the sack and felt its contents. While he lifted out the urn and examined it, I looked at the swastikas and the graffiti sprayed on the walls of the hotel and on the memorial to the Alpine regiment.

"Yes," the man said, lifting the urn to his ear, "we are looking for the guilty. A lot of work is needed to clean up that mess."

While he shook the urn, Josie stood with arms akimbo and leaned forward.

"Be careful with that," she snapped. "It's not, like, a paint spray. It's an urn, and it contains our father's ashes."

Glancing upwards, the soldier caught the full force of Josie's withering stare.

"It was his wish that his ashes be scattered above *Oberwald*, yeah?"

"The scattering of ashes is not allowed in Germany," the soldier said, handing the urn to Josie. "Lucky for you I haven't time for this."

"No worries."

We watched him walk towards our hotel. His hunched shoulders and tilted head suggested he was walking into a strong wind and prompted Josie and I to put on our cagoules. When the military man was out of sight, we set off up the mountain.

Accepting that an ascent of the *Widderstein* would be foolhardy, we decided to walk to the hut at the foot of this great obelisk and scatter the ashes there. I was in tip-top condition despite Ben's claim that I was the wrinkliest daddy in his school and despite the assumption voiced by several school mums that I was a proud grandfather. I hoped to make good time in the cool of the morning and estimated that 1000 metres would take us about 3 hours.

After about an hour, we were well up the valley, but I knew I had underestimated the task in front of us. Not only was Josie lagging behind, but my heart was thumping, my calf muscles straining and the straps of the rucksack were rubbing into my shoulders. Father's novel was also reminding me of its presence by poking its edges into my back.

*The White Mountain* had accompanied me in one shape or form since childhood but it played a very significant role in my life when my father left us. At first, he kept in contact by posting stories to me about Black Patch the pirate and his escapades in the coastal town of West Wittering. Every morning, I would rush to the door when I heard the plop of envelopes dropping on the doormat. The brown paper my father employed to wrap my stories was easy to spot and, if I was lucky

4

enough to find such a packet on the doormat, I would scurry off to my room and read its contents in private.

Around 1961, when my father met his second wife, the plopping of letters on the doormat brought only bills and disappointments. Unable to accept that my father would forget me, I scoured the pages of *The White Mountain* for mention of boys who battled pirates in a town called West Wittering. This was no easy task for a 9-year-old boy who needed to know his father had not abandoned him. But instead of the words "Black Patch" or "West Wittering" he found only swirls and dots on a page. As his reading skills improved, he studied the book for some message from his father that might explain why he had gone away. The book gave the boy nothing but riddles and peculiar place names. There was a region known as the "Dolomite Alps," a village called "*Quero Vas*," and geographical features like the "Valley of the Prisoners" and the "Valley of Heroes." There was no mention of pirates living in West Wittering, but there was a village policeman and his girlfriend. Both had names the boy could not pronounce: Sergio and Beatrice.

The weather deteriorated soon after we reached a point about 500 metres above the *Kreuzberg*. The late summer morning seemed to promise the arrival of winter, and it began to rain. A restless wind pulled at my rucksack and disturbed my walking rhythm. The air was damp to my face and the valley was full of sound. Icy rain pitter-pattered against my cagoule, and the chill stream beside us rushed and tumbled. Its water was as black as the clouds that now hung over us, and gusts of wind picked up the spray and threw it in my face.

After another hour, we entered a forest, and the path turned away from the stream. With the protection of the trees, we plunged into a world of silence and pines. Their perfume filled the air, and their needles softened the ground under my feet. But no amount of shifting or wriggling of shoulders prevented *The White Mountain* from prodding the small of my back.

Its presence brought to mind our meeting with father's former literary agent 2 months previously. I found that I was inhaling to the rhythm of his words: "It's all in his books, all in his books," and exhaling to the rhythm of: "It was a purging experience, a purging experience." The novel was with us because we hoped its contents would provide evidence that father had been writing about his experiences in *Oberwald* in 1939. If the book had been a purging experience, we wanted to know what our father was guilty of and whether the book was a confession.

Absorbed with these questions, I did not notice that the rain had turned to snow, and a layer of white was covering the pine needles. From time to time one of us stepped on a twig or a branch, and the birds in the trees took flight, and lumps of snow fell on our heads or cagoules. Occasionally, I caught sight of the *Widderstein*. Hovering over us, its peak was set hard against the cloud; but sometimes, its summit wind pulled at the snow, hurled it around the crags, and the mountain disappeared from view.

Josie and I took a breather just below the ridge that led to the foot of the *Widderstein*. Josie slumped against the rock face and hung her head. Jets of vapour poured from her nostrils and drifted over her in clouds. She raised her head, and her eyes gazed into mine. They flickered from side to side as if she was reading my thoughts. I pulled off my gloves, turned my head away from her and stared at our footprints in the snow. These signs of our passing trailed away into the forest, and my thoughts touched upon the possibility that we should follow them and go down. When I looked at Josie again, her eyes were still and there was a satisfied expression on her face that seemed to say, "You're afraid," but before I could utter a word, Josie made a decision for both of us.

"What's up, Nick? Aren't you up for it?"

The crunch of trainers on snow announced her departure, and I strode after her, the cagoule flapping against my thighs.

It had stopped snowing when we reached the ridge. At 2,500 metres, it curved away to meet an upland plateau where, at a distance that seemed hand-touchingly close, the walkers' hut was waiting for us. I was struck by a sense of familiarity – a trace of memory trying to surface. Josie lurched up to me. She bent double, trying to catch her wind by sucking the oxygen from every beat of her heart. Eventually, with words that ran on a breath, she said:

"We have a photo of this hut, don't we?"

She lifted her arm to indicate the place she was referring to but it fell back and swung loosely beside her. I scanned the world in front of me while Josie pulled more air into her lungs. Faraway and beyond the trees, *Oberwald* was visible as a miniature of glistening colour where everything looked as new as spring. The forest stretched out below us, and its upper reaches were shrouded in snow.

As soon as Josie had regained her breath, I said:

"We do have a photo. Look."

I had intended to draw Josie's attention to the features of the mountains and to the position and shape of the walkers' hut. I was going to suggest that this place was indeed the hut depicted in one of my father's photos and that it was the hut that had fired my imagination as a child. I turned with my arm outstretched, my finger pointing. I expected to see the *Widderstein* and the ridge behind me. I stepped backwards. Tentacles of white were lapping around the ridge we were to follow.

Unheard and unseen, the cloud had crept up behind us. The *Widderstein* and the hut with no name had disappeared from view.

"We'd better try and make for the shelter of the refuge," I said, backing away from the swirling cloud. It appeared to me as the entrance to another world and, from the valley below, the church bell tolled. Its sound was resonant like a death knell and although it filled me with dread, it was Josie who verbalised my fears.

"Is that cool?"

I rested my hand on her elbow and gripped it to let the pulse of confidence flow into her, but she turned her head away from mine, her apprehension rippling down her jaw and coming to a stop as a throb in her neck.

"It's not like we have a choice, right?"

"It's impossible to lose our way."

I settled my rucksack on my shoulders and plunged into the world of whiteness. At first, I heard Josie's breathing from behind but the ridge we were following was sharp and narrow, and soon we were stumbling. I could not see where the snow finished or where the cloud began, and the smallest rock seemed there to trip me. I felt forward motion but saw no movement, and there was no sound save the panting of my breath and the rustling of the rucksack against my back.

I stopped and looked around.

I was alone.

Closing my eyes, I turned my head from side to side but the world was wrapped in a snowy silence. My eyes were only half-open when the mist lifted for an instant and, as though a stage curtain had been drawn back, I caught a glimpse of the hut. It was much closer than I had thought, and I wondered if Josie had overtaken me. Then, the mist fell again; and the curtain was snatched shut.

I peered into the damp and swirling air. It gave rise to

transient shapes but it was only when there was another momentary breach in the mist that I caught a glimpse of Josie. She was on her knees and digging into her rucksack. Sensing my presence, she looked towards me in the manner of a man who had been caught with his trousers down. Before either of us could say a word, the breach closed and Josie vanished. I edged towards her, and her face was suddenly there in front of mine. She said:

"Why have we come? We've come to bury him, haven't we?"

The snow had stopped falling, but the mist rose and fell over us. I wondered whether Josie had suffered a breakdown of some kind. She seemed to have forgotten my presence and was pulling out the contents of her rucksack and muttering to herself. Blood was trickling down her temple. It was dripping onto the snow and forming red stars.

"Damn you, damn you," Josie said.

She stood up, gripped the urn in her hands and shook it.

"He's still here, right?"

Losing her balance, she fell to her knees and slammed the urn down on the snow.

"Away," she said. "I want him away."

I supposed Josie had slipped and hit her head but I broke into a cold sweat when I guessed she was suffering from concussion. I tried to focus on the here and now and how I would get her off the mountain. I knelt down beside her. Picking up the urn, I said:

"Josie, Josie. Not like this."

I slipped the urn into the side pocket of my rucksack and put my arm around her shoulders.

"Josie," I said. "We need to get out of here."

"He's still here. He's still with us."

I put my arm under hers and helped her to her feet,

but she stood like a sleepwalker that nobody could wake. She said:

"Why are we here?"

"To scatter the ashes, Josie. We've come to scatter father's ashes."

She was shivering from head to foot, and her lips were blue. She suddenly broke away from me and, setting off up the ridge, she fell to her knees and toppled forward onto the snow.

"Josie, Josie..."

She pushed herself up, got to her feet and brushed past me. Stumbling down the ridge, she muttered something over her shoulder and faded into the mist. Then, from close at hand came a shout. I turned an ear into the cold and damp world and, as the snow began falling again, I heard the shout for a second time. The mist was breaking into drifting patches and, between the patches, a disorderly and irregular shape was heading in my direction. At first, came a blue outline. Then came an ice-axe and scarves wrapped like bandages round a face and head. I muttered a few words of thanks to myself. Half-buried in snow, Josie was just a few metres away from me and lying on her back.

"Over here," I shouted.

"I'm a doctor," the man said.

We slid down the slope towards Josie, lifted her to her feet and dragged her back up to the ridge. I grabbed at her rucksack, and the three of us cursed our way through the snow until the silhouette of a hut revealed itself. In the mist, the hut seemed two dimensional and I got the impression that if I opened the door I would burst through the wall and onto a stage set. My companion curled his hand around the doorknob, twisted his wrist, and we crashed inside.

I half-expected to find the hut peopled by figures from my childhood imagination. My father, for example, would be waiting for us with his blond-haired lover while his enemy, Christian Von Stoutenberg, prowled around outside. I could almost see my father offering us a hot drink and I heard him greeting us with the words, "What took you so long?"

But we were greeted only by silence, and the hut was empty and the air was thick with dust. I squinted at the brick walls and the archways which stretched out in front of me and which divided the interior into three sections. At the far end of the hut, beckoning us with a promise of warmth and life, a fire burned. We manhandled Josie down a rickety flight of steps and my companion said:

"She is too cold. We must hurry."

We frogmarched her into the first section of the room and we passed piles of bricks on which planks lay to form makeshift tables and benches. Everything seemed covered in a layer of powder and cobwebs.

"It is lucky for us you came," I said. "Without you, I think we'd be in desperate trouble."

"I saw you on the ridge. When you did not come, I knew something was wrong."

Entry into the second section was marked by an oil lamp hanging from a rotting beam and a primus stove standing on a table. We hauled Josie past these and into an odour of terminal dampness. A few cables dangled from the right-hand wall and, between them, decades of graffiti stood our clearly and preserved the presence of walkers from times gone by.

"On any other day," my companion said, "even yesterday or tomorrow – the hut would have been empty."

The second section was separated from the third by a sheet of tarpaulin, which had been tied from one wall to the other. The tarpaulin hung under the ceiling and collected the rain and snow that fell through holes in the

11

roof. Drops of water hit the tarpaulin with a continuous plop.

Eventually we dropped Josie in a chair by the fire and we covered her with a blanket.

"What are we doing here?" Josie mumbled.

"She asks a good question," said the man. "The weather is so bad. What in God's name are you doing up here – and without proper clothes?"

His lips barely disturbed the scarves that wrapped his head, and his angry words appeared to have come from another place. I allowed my eyes to drift upwards from his mouth, past the opening for his nose and then to his eyes. We exchanged a long and silent stare.

"Scattering these ashes," I said.

"Why here?"

"It was his last wish."

"And why on this day of all days? Did you not know the risks?"

I took off my rucksack and drew the urn out of its side pocket.

"We had no choice," I said.

*

The log fire has long since ceased to glimmer, but dots of light dance in front of my eyes, and I think the darkness might be easing. Either I am seeing the low archways or they are being conjured up by a mix of wishful thinking and associations with the odour of dampness and with the water plip-plopping on the tarpaulin sheet. I have lost any sense of passing time and, in this stillness, other fears are finding their voices. They are telling me that Josie and I should have left the past in peace and that we might be about to receive the penalty we deserve.

The focus of my fears and the reason I cannot allow

myself to fall asleep is the other man. He says he is a doctor but I have no evidence of this. He seemed competent when he examined Josie and dressed her wound last night. My worry is that after our long talk, he guessed at the truth. He might decide to hurt us. Does he have a gun or a knife? Maybe he has a springy truncheon like the ones I saw yesterday during the riot. He is no more than 3 metres from me. If he wakes up, I will hear him. If he decides on vengeance, I will have time to prepare myself.

It is true that we had no choice. Our arrival in this hut was dictated by events that occurred many years before Josie and I were born. It was our father who decided that his ashes were to be scattered on this day and on this mountain, but I knew nothing of this until I met Josie 4 months ago on the occasion of our father's funeral.

## 2

Although I tried to find one, there was no excuse for arriving late at the funeral service. Fortunately, I did not need that lost time to cry or mourn or say my last goodbye because I had already done these things as a child, but I was trying to slip unseen into the chapel when the squeaky door betrayed my late arrival. I was caught red-handed. Blank faces turned in my direction, and eyes glared at me as though I had been committing an indecent act.

I closed the door with a degree of care that suggested I was not as boorish as my lateness implied. Shrinking down on a pew, I realised I could not even claim that father's death was unexpected. When any man reaches his late eighties, his imminent death can hang over you for years. His coffin had been brought in; the other mourners had already formed a tight group, and the celebrant was in full flow.

"He began my creation with constraint," he was saying, "by giving me life he added only confusion. We depart reluctantly still not knowing the aim of birth, existence, and departure."

While burying my head in the order of service, I reflected on the words of the celebrant and how nice it was that he should quote from the writings of Omar Khayyam. Sadly, I had missed the entrance music, but the choice of song – "Somewhere over the Rainbow" – was a surprise. I saw no relationship between it and the verses of a Persian poet, and I associated neither with my father.

I turned back to the front cover. I barely recognised the man portrayed in the photograph, but the title – "A celebration of the life of Charles Saddler: 1920 – 2010" - reassured me that I had, at least, not compounded my embarrassment by gate-crashing someone else's service.

"Charles Saddler was a very private man," the celebrant intoned. "He was also a man of conviction. He never liked to be the centre of attention but his books drew us to him."

The celebrant was a large round man in a tight black suit. He had a fleshy face and a large bottom lip which hung like the rim of a milk jug and which could not quite deal with the difference between the letters /r/ and /w/.

"In life and now in death," he continued, "he wouldn't want us to focus on him. He wouldn't want us to focus on the sadness of his death, but instead to focus on what he has left behind for posterity. In a sense, he lives on in his books."

A man was sitting several rows in front of me. His inclined head and hunched shoulders suggested he was expecting to be attacked from behind. Both his hands, resting on the pew in front of him, shook. The aisle separated both of us from the tight group on our right. The neat rows of black veils and dabbing white handkerchiefs were disturbed by fidgety children and a man in a white t-shirt. He was staring at the coffin with a supercilious grin that seemed to say: "To hell with you."

A scattering of my father's genes revealed those of

the group who were close family members. One of the group, a woman of about thirty-five, had more of father's genes than the others. A huge ball of frizzy dark hair suggested attitude and, in that room of dark sobriety, her red and green striped tights drew attention to her. The black tie, although appropriate in the setting of a funeral, had been thrown over her neck, and the knot came to rest - a full stop on the flesh – beneath the collars of an open shirt.

"A man as focused as Charles Saddler was never an easy person to live with," the celebrant said. "And yet, he loved his children and grandchildren more than he was able to show. Although we will miss him, his smile, his love, we take consolation in the good feelings of our memories."

The lady in the red and green tights turned her back on the mourners beside her, stretched her legs into the aisle and crossed them. While one leg swung over the other, she regarded the celebrant with a facial expression that suggested she was watching a film which neither bored nor interested her. Both her expression and her clothes seemed designed to grab the attention of others. I was wondering who these other people might be when the celebrant looked at her and said:

"You remember that Christmas, don't you, Josie?"

The lady nodded and lowered her head while a pulse of energy ran through her arms, and she shivered as if at the sight or sound of something unpleasant.

"Josie was having a very hard time waiting for Christmas morning. She thought it would never come. After days of waiting, it finally got the best of her. There she sat on the living room carpet, huge tears rolling down her cheeks. Her dad didn't even ask what the matter was. He simply picked her up, tucked his daughter into his lap and told her not to worry because Christmas always comes. That's the way Charles

Saddler was. He was intuitive. He somehow knew what to say and what to do, even in those times when you had not spoken. And though he knew what to say in his books, in so many ways, he was a man of few spoken words. You could always count on one important thing, though. Whatever he said, though the words were not expansive, they were the right words."

The eulogy disappointed me. What did this celebrant know of right words? Why did he not mention the effects of words' absence - a telephone that never rang; the letterless mat by the front door?

"Many of you knew Charles Saddler as a strong and proud man, but he was quiet and reserved as well. In many of his books, he showed sympathy for the oppressed, the outsider and the downtrodden but sympathy was not necessarily a trait that he displayed to all who knew him. It was not his fault. He lived at a time - the great depression, the war - where sympathy and compassion were not always the way to survive. And his own father had already impressed upon him the seriousness of life, its duties and obligations and the necessity of discipline. There was no time for the finer qualities of life in those early years for Charles Saddler."

The man with the supercilious grin folded his arms and exchanged whispers with a sad-eyed woman beside him. My half-sibling, Josie, turned. The upward tilt of her chin obliged her to stare down her nose at them, and the couple fell silent. I got the impression that Josie would not tolerate any disruptions in her life. It occurred to me that this disruption might include the arrival of a long-lost older brother like me.

"Possibly due to that early upbringing, Charles was disciplined in his work and in his life. His name is still known to readers of thrillers and his family is proud of him, of all that he was, and all that maybe he would have liked to be if times had been different."

As the coffin rolled towards the curtains, it shuddered and stopped. A ripple of excitement disturbed the group to my right. Heads bobbed and eyes stared, and the man with the grin crouched forward. He looked ready to spring up, run down the aisle and thump the person responsible for this hiccough.

Fortunately, the blip was temporary, and the coffin set off again. This time it was accompanied by a crackle as of frying eggs. From the crackle emerged a melody, a song from the depths of my father's history. The man with the inclined head and hunched shoulders leaned forward. A lock of white hair tumbled over his forehead and covered the hands that now held his face. I guessed from the movement of his shoulders that the man was sobbing.

The song was in German, and the lyrics were printed in the booklet with an English translation. The singing voice was a falsetto from a bygone time.

> Come back, I am waiting for you because you are my happiness.
> Come back, my heart cries always out for you for you are my destiny.
> Even if it takes a long time it will lead you and me to bliss.
> So, I beg you today: Come back.

The music and words from my father's formative years prompted in me a surprising twinge of loss. Although I had come to understand my parents in the context of their own lives, the song and the time it represented were beyond the experience of those left behind. "You see," my father seemed to be saying, "there was a time before you, and I was living then. Today, that time is out of your reach. You had your chance to ask me about it, and that chance is now gone."

Perhaps, he had foreseen the effects that total absence might have on his children. Absence cannot speak; absence has its secrets that can longer be shared. And in that moment, the twinge of loss surged to such a peak that the desire to halt the progress of the coffin towards the flames was unsparing. "Come back," I almost shouted. "Please, come back. I have some questions. I need to know what life was like for you. What did you feel about it? Come back."

It was too late to expect answers from a body that was about to disappear in a cloud of smoke, and then the crackle of the record stopped with an electronic clunk.

"Nick?"

I looked up. I was alone in the chapel.

"Nick? You're alright now, yeah?"

I span round and into a cloud of tears. Josie was standing at the open door. Smoke from her cigarette was wafting into the chapel. She had cupped one elbow in the palm of her hand and held the offending cigarette at her ear. She turned her head upwards and glared at me as if daring me to challenge her. I swiped at my eyes with thumb and forefinger and, walking towards the door and the sunlight, I waved my hands in a gesture of smoke-dispersal and frowned my way past her.

"Please, call me Nicholas," I said.

Several metres from the chapel, I stopped at a fork in the path. The left-hand fork led to a garden area while the right-hand fork led to the car park. Another funeral service was about to take place. Other mourners were gathering, other tears being cried, and another hearse had crept up and stood waiting between the car park and the chapel. There was a voice from behind.

"How was it for you, Nicholas?"

I acknowledged her question with a shake of the head. Big brothers were not supposed to cry.

"Shall we get away from here?" I suggested.

Without turning, I strode along the left-hand path until I found myself amongst large open lawns, flowering trees, shrubs and rose beds. Without noticing, I had slipped into the garden of remembrance. Plaques sat with the rose bushes and others topped the logs that flanked the pathways. When my eyes had cleared, I said:

"How was what for me, by the way?"

I noticed a hint of irritation in my voice and wondered why it was there. Josie had, after all, taken the trouble to find me on the internet. This must have required a degree of persistence. She had eventually found me at the History department at King Edward's College, University of London. If Josie had not been persistent, she would not have been able to inform me of father's death. Nor would she have been able to inform me of the funeral arrangements.

"Having a second-rate scribbler as a dad?" she said.

She appeared at my shoulder, and we walked in silence until we reached a magnolia tree. I pretended to admire the budding flowers while I considered my response.

"Can't really say," I said.

"Didn't you notice?"

I shook my head.

"I was eight when he left."

"He did his usual disappearing trick, did he?"

"He turned up from time to time."

"From time to time? Cool. Sounds just like dad."

The well-tended lawn, soft beneath my feet, swept away towards the car park. Several groups were gathering there. Those who had yet to go through the chapel doors were easy to spot. They were characterised by bowed heads and handkerchiefs, and hands held in greeting or condolence. Members of our group were standing in a large circle, twirling car keys around their fingers and backing off towards their cars. Occasionally, their voices drifted towards us on a breeze.

"We'll follow you," said one voice.

"To the house, then," said another.

"Father was not with us in person," I said, "but his reputation was – especially when *The White Mountain* was published. After that, nobody asked me about him."

"He was a bit of a one-hit wonder, wasn't he? Did your mother talk about him?"

"She didn't bring up the subject that much."

"Your mother's still alive?"

"Yes."

She looked at me reflectively.

"Your mother and dad met in Italy, didn't they?"

"That's right," I said.

My parents had met in Verona, and I, their only son, was born there in 1952. I was seven when we returned to England, and memories of Italy often came to me with the smell of olive oil or of grappa and appeared as still-life images of shadows breaking over forgotten courtyards, porticos, and squares. My mother told me that I had been completely bilingual in Italy but by the time I had been back in England for 3 years, my Italian had gone.

"And they separated when?"

"I think it was 1960."

I used the word "think" to indicate indifference towards the event itself. The truth was that I knew both the month and the year. It was July 1960. The Shadows were playing on the wireless, and my father's disappearance from my life was forevermore associated with the beating drums of "Apache."

"It must have been difficult," she said.

"Eight-year-olds are very resilient."

And I found resilience wherever I could. I believed my mother when she told me my father would come home one day. My mother said that his new wife would not let him come and live with us just yet. As the years passed, and I became inquisitive, she told me he was an impossible man, and if I needed to know why I should ask him directly or read his books. I also found resilience in my father's shadow and I held on to it for years. The shadow arrived in my life when I was about 6 years old and I discovered the inevitability of death. To give father full credit, he did not try to deny it. He told me that one day he would die but that he would never go away completely. If ever I wanted to see him, he said, I should walk in the sunlight. He would always be there in the shadow beside me.

"When we were growing up, dad never mentioned his first marriage."

"I can imagine," I said.

And imagination was all I had to go on. When my father remarried in 1963, he withdrew from my life. I visited him on several occasions in his Wiltshire house but I always felt unwanted. My father would shut himself away in his writing room, and I hardly ever saw him. His second wife was pleasant enough, but like a nurse, which she had been, she attended to my needs with a smile but emotionally, she had cut herself off. She was Roman Catholic and probably found me an unwelcome reminder that her husband was divorced. None of this was my fault, but at the time I felt dirty. When I was fourteen, and the Rolling Stones were singing "As Tears Go by," I told my mother that I no longer wanted to visit my father. It was also at this time that I gave up searching for him in my shadow. Instead, I found him in his books and some personal items that had turned up in his sock drawer soon after he left us.

"I was nineteen when dad told me I had a half-brother," Josie said. "Can you believe that?"

"I guess he just wanted to start a new life."

Josie shuffled uncomfortably, snapped her bag open

and pulled out her pack of Players.

"But he took care of you, didn't he?"

"I hardly ever saw him."

She was standing close to my shoulder, holding an unlit cigarette at her ear and flicking nervously at the filter with her thumb.

"But he, like, paid maintenance, yeah?"

"My mother never told me," I said. "I suppose he did."

"No worries, then."

But her hand was unsteady when she reached into her bag, extracted the packet of Players and slid the unlit cigarette back into its place. She turned her head towards a pathway leading through the light and shadow of woodland adjacent to the lawns. A man emerged from between the trees and came towards us. I recognised him as the old man who had attended the service. The lock of white hair was now brushed back and revealed a forehead divided by two parallel and vertical folds of skin. The eyes beneath these folds were those of a tired hunting dog and they rested on us as he approached. He acknowledged our presence with a slight nod of the head and then passed on.

"What will you do with the ashes?"

"We are under strict orders, yeah?"

"To do what?"

"To scatter them on some God-forsaken mountain in the Bavarian Alps."

"Oh, I see," I said.

"Any ideas why?" she asked.

I would never have described myself as a secretive person but information was power, and the contents of an old paper bag in my jacket pocket were my information and my power and I would choose my moment to reveal them.

"Not really, I'm afraid."

"No worries."

"They say he gave up writing in 1991," I said. "What made him stop so early?"

"Does that matter? Does anyone, like, care why a book is never written?"

"It just seemed so sudden."

"Think so? Maybe he reached a point in his life when he didn't care enough."

"About what?"

"About what people thought of him. Around 1990 he acted as if other people, like, simply did not exist for him. Or perhaps the people whose opinions he valued were no longer there."

"So – did something happen in 1991 to force this change?"

"Not that we are aware of. He moved down to Ottermouth in 1991 but that would hardly be reason to stop writing, would it?"

"Can't say," I said.

"We'd better go."

She must have seen me hesitate. She added, "You are coming, aren't you? To dad's house, I mean. For the reception?"

She frowned into my silence and said:

"There's something I want you to see."

"Oh, yes?"

"It came this morning – a mystery item from New York. It's quite cool really."

"What's the mystery, then?"

She took a step away from me, folded her arms and looked me straight in the eyes.

"This thing from New York. It's from the dark and long silence, probably."

"Sorry," I said, "you've lost me."

"The dark and long silence? That period of dad's life before his children were born."

"A period to which 'Somewhere over the Rainbow' and other songs belong."

"Quite."

"Is that why you chose them?"

"Dad organised the whole event, yeah? We know nothing about his choice of songs."

"And this thing from New York?"

"Beyond the experience of anyone we know."

"By the way," I said, "who was that old man?"

"Which old man?"

"The one who passed us a while ago."

"No idea," Josie said.

"Strange," I said. "But old men never seem out of place near memorials to the dead."

\*

About 4 months have passed since I made Josie's acquaintance that day of the cremation. I recall my reaction to her and to her clothes and I now know whose attention she was trying to grab. I understand now because she and I are from the same mould and I should have recognised her behaviour in my own.

For me, it started when I was 14 years old and I observed my best friend's relationship with his father. It was not simply that his dad came to rugby matches or the school play. I noticed that they shared in life so profoundly that it created a longing in me. From that time on, I did everything to get my father's imaginary approval. When I acted in the school play, I would picture the perfect dad watch me turn on a performance that brought the house down. When I played rugby, my father would be in my mind when I scored the winning try. When I got married for the first time in 1982, my imaginary father was still with me and he was there in the church to applaud his perfectly dressed son and his perfect bride.

I see now that my behaviour was not so very different from Josie's. In a sense, her clothes and behaviour on the day of the funeral added up to the best tribute she could have paid to her father. She was doing what she had always done. Even on the occasion of his funeral, she was trying to get his attention.

# 3

The night passes. Dark against the darkness, the outline of the space that encloses me appears. Someone makes a sound. I strain my ears, and my eyes dance and flicker but I am unable to pinpoint the source. Disembodied words drift towards me. I suppose they are whispers, but in the silence, they sound like trumpet blasts.

"Be happy now and don't live on wind."

It is Josie speaking in her sleep. The words are clearly enunciated, and I recognise them as one line of a verse from the *Rubaiyat* of Omar Khayyam. The complete verse was written on a postcard in 1939 and presented by my father to his lover as an expression of everlasting devotion. The card reappeared on the day of my father's cremation. It was attached to Josie's "thing" from the dark and long silence.

This "thing" turned out to be a large wreath and it temporarily united Charles Saddler's five children that afternoon after the service. There were other wreaths on the dining table, but the New York wreath was different. It was the unknown drawing us all towards it.

*

I was abandoned as soon as I crossed the threshold of father's house. Josie, my link with this after-the-cremation event, had indicated where I could find the New York wreath and disappeared with my coat. Left alone in the entrance hall, I was attracted by a babble of voices coming from the heart of the house and I was edging towards it when I was waylaid by items of furniture. I had not them since my father left, and they prompted fragments of memory. Disconnected from place or time, these memories were somehow associated with my father: the smell of his dressing gown, the way he would roll his eyes and remove his glasses, the snug fit of my hand in his.

I was lost in this sensory world when I felt a presence at my side.

"Hello?"

The greeting was followed by silence and emptiness where an outstretched hand might have presented itself for me to shake.

"I'm Tony. I'm an architect."

While taking in the gap between us, I stared down at my half-brother's domed pate and his black-rimmed glasses. I considered picking up the gauntlet and engaging him in the my-status-is-in-my-job game, but decided against it. The word "architect" was crisp and loaded with confident consonants. In contrast, the words "university" and "lecturer" sounded limp and ineffectual.

"Nicholas," I said.

At the end of the hallway, open double doors revealed an alcove and a large table adorned with sunny wreaths and flowers. The New York wreath was easy to spot. So much bigger than its rivals, it was a vibrant mass of colour and petals and had no discernible beginning or end. Tony the architect cast a smile over his face but the eyes behind the glasses were brimming with suspicion.

"Glad you made it to the funeral?"

"I liked the music," I said. "I suppose 'Somewhere over the Rainbow' was his favourite song."

"Whose favourite song?"

"Father's."

Tony let his eyelids flicker and momentarily closed them before saying:

"Dad used to hum it occasionally."

He turned his head sideways to me and said to nobody in particular:

"Why don't you circulate - just barge in and introduce yourself to the others."

Several people were flitting in and out of eyeshot. From upstairs came the sound of children enjoying their freedom after the restraints of the service. Gleeful shouts and bumps on the ceiling brought a black look to Tony's face. For me, it was a pleasing affirmation of life after the funeral.

"Everyone'll be delighted to meet you," Tony said.

He swung away from me, but I followed. We edged and stepped a passage through the double doors and towards the table in the alcove. We must have resembled a couple performing some ritualistic dance, but I was not going to let Tony go. With Josie away, he was my link with this family, and he gave me some legitimacy. I was struggling to find a topic that might connect us. Talking about football or the weather seemed inappropriate at a man's wake.

"I particularly liked the song at the end of the service," I said. "Did father play a lot of German music? Did he speak German?"

Tony tutted my question aside and said:

"Just don't stand on ceremony. Nobody bites."

29

Stretching his cheeks into an imitation smile, he slipped off towards the kitchen. I came to rest on the sidelines beside the large table. The guests were standing in small groups. Heads nodded, glasses were raised and voices murmured. Josie had already informed me about my fellow mourners. After absorbing the names of my other half-siblings: Miriam, Petra and Tony, my mind had wandered, and the names of their spouses, children, and in-laws dispersed in the air before I could properly assimilate them. To make matters more complicated, Josie had added colourful sketches to several names before signing them off with a one-word caption. Amongst these captions were the words "sad" and "tosser." I was now left with the task of fitting barely remembered names and captions with people and putting them together like the pieces of a jig-saw puzzle.

From the babble of voices, detached scraps of conversation reached out to me.

"Yes, wasn't it nice?"

"He would've liked it the way it was."

"Well, he had a good innings."

"So passes away earthly glory; cool."

Silence.

A face swept out of the crowd and paused in front of me. Tony's wife, Hilary, was bringing round the finger food.

"Mustn't linger," she said. "I've got two hungry brothers to attend to."

She plunged into the gathering, and I followed her progress by watching the plate of sandwiches. Held over her head, it was as conspicuous as a beacon. I watched the beacon rise and dip over unknown shapes and shadows until it rocked to a halt and hovered over two men on a sofa. They were nodding to the movements of Hilary's talking head and, as though in response to a signal, they turned indifferent eyes in my direction and made a movement of the hands that suggested a wave.

The sad-eyed lady from the chapel appeared with a tray of drinks.

"I'm Nicholas."

"Petra," she replied. "There are lots of thirsty people to deal with, including my family. I've got three kids, you know - two children and my husband Tom."

My half-sister rolled her eyes and offered me a crooked smile but by the time she dived into the other guests, I thought her eyes had contained an appeal for a lifeline. She resurfaced by the side of two children who were playing at a man's feet. I recognised him immediately as the man in the chapel with the supercilious grin. Petra bent over him in the manner of a servile waiter looking for a tip before hurrying away to join two elderly couples shuffling in a corner and trying hard not to interfere.

Occasionally, a barked order would fly out of the kitchen and whizz past my ear. Through a process of elimination, I guessed that this commanding voice belonged to the director of the afternoon's activities, my half-sister Miriam.

"I suppose Josie told you about the ashes."

Tony had arrived by my side. The expression in his eyes and the hardness around his jaw implied I was responsible for my father's decision with regard to his ashes.

"Yes," I said.

"Then you know that Dad asked for his ashes to be scattered in Germany."

I raised my eyebrows and smiled in a way that was designed to suggest I knew something he did not.

"She did mention it," I said.

"What's so special about Germany?" Tony hissed. "D'you know?"

I did not like Tony's tone and I was going to show

this individual that university lecturers were not as ineffectual as the sound of the words suggested.

"This wreath's really enormous, isn't it?"

I leaned forward to examine it. I recognised white lilies and chrysanthemums but there were blue and violet alpine-looking plants that I could not name. Not only did its size and vibrant colours set it apart from the other wreaths, it was also lying askew. Its envelope contained a card, but both wreath and card seemed somehow neglected. The other cards had been propped up neatly to claim possession of their owners.

"So, do you know why dad asked for his ashes to be...?"

"I'm really sorry," I said. "I'm afraid I've no idea."

I leaned forward to pick up the envelope.

"By the way," I said, "do you know why father stopped writing so early?"

"Perhaps," said a woman's voice, "he came to see how inadequate words were."

I looked up. Tony had crept away, and Petra had replaced him. She was flushed and distracted, and her eyes constantly flickered over to her husband, Tom, and their two children.

"After all," she said, "there are feelings that cannot be translated into words of any language, aren't there?"

Holding the envelope between thumb and forefinger, I followed the direction of Petra's flickering glances and found a colourful object. Josie was flitting about from shadow to shadow. She engaged everybody with expansive movements of the arms, the intensity of which seemed to signal the depth of her feelings. Occasionally, these movements bordered on the absurd. It occurred to me that perhaps these gestures were intended to draw attention and Josie's way of saying that she was a warm and agreeable person. She eventually came to rest on the arm of a chair. She threw one red and green leg over the other and used them both to compete with Petra's children for their father's attention.

"For example?"

"Things like the nature of love or of hate."

"Or jealousy," I said on impulse and immediately regretted it. The brief flicker on Petra's bottom lip was more than an appeal for a lifeline; it was a cry for help. A few seconds passed, and then she said:

"Maybe, he could no longer get his novels published. He never matched the success of *The White Mountain*, did he?"

I slid the card from the envelope and span it round in my fingers. I was expecting to see a card from some long-lost relative like me – the sort of person whose name or presence brought an awkward atmosphere to proceedings.

"You think he just ran out of steam?" I said.

But Petra had gone on the offensive. I watched her bending over her children while she made a side comment to Tom that floored him and sent Josie fluttering away.

Something white fell out of the envelope and dropped onto the desk. It was a small plant with white oblong leaves and a tuft of floral leaves surrounding the flowers.

"Looks like edelweiss. Dried," said a crisp voice from behind.

Miriam had emerged from her kitchen command post and stood with her legs together and her feet pointing outwards at 10 minutes to two.

"You must be Nicholas."

Her voice carried hints of a parade-ground order, its tone reaching a crescendo on the first syllable of my name. There followed a collective hush, a lapse into silence, as if the guests were listening out for danger. Perhaps they thought I had come to pick over the inheritance.

"Yes, it is a high mountain plant," Miriam said. "As you know, not many plants can survive the night frosts and the summer sun."

She could have been carrying on a conversation with an old friend and she picked up the plant, grabbed my elbow with one hand and slipped the edelweiss into the envelope with the other.

"Good man," she said. "These plants don't lose their attractiveness after drying, do they?"

"So why would anyone send this?"

"It symbolises courage, purity and love," said another voice. It was accompanied by a hand which alighted on my upper arm. It was removed immediately. Josie must have felt me flinch.

"It's considered a symbol of bravery," she said. "It's often dangerous to get them from the high crags. The flowers are then presented by the man to his beloved. Cool, isn't it?"

Miriam glanced at Josie and became restive. Something had breached her standards of conduct. She raised a finger and wagged it between disapproving eyebrows.

"Taboo," she cried, and clipped away into the kitchen.

Josie seemed on the point of responding but raised her arms in a gesture of helplessness. She nodded at the card I was turning between my fingers.

"The edelweiss is not the only mystery that came with the wreath," she said. "Makes you wonder what dad got up to when he was young, doesn't it? And what are all these sudden connections to Germany? We knew nothing about them until we read the obituary."

"Obituary?"

"Nothing grand. Just some paragraphs, yeah? In *The West Country Gazette*."

"You said the wreath came from New York."

34

"It did," Josie said. "But the edelweiss and the card attached to it are clearly connected to Germany. Have a look at the card. Go on, it's cool, really."

The card was worn and cracked like a piece of old ceramic. On one side, it displayed a black and white shot of the mountains. *Oberwald* was written at the bottom, along with the name *Kreuzberg*. *Kreuzberg* seemed to be one of two smaller mountains that rose above the town. The photo had been taken at a time when cloud was lifting from the summit. The white summit obelisk, catching a ray of morning sunlight, shone brightly through the dispersing mist and seemed to hang in the air. I flicked the card over.

To N with love from CS. August 1939.
Don't seek to recall yesterday that is past
Nor repine for tomorrow which has yet to come;
Don't build your hopes on the past or the future
Be happy now and don't live on wind.

I studied the writing for some time. It was neat and right-slanted and curved upwards at the end of each line. There were large gaps between each letter. I recognised the lines immediately and was on the point of telling Josie when there was a rallying cry from Miriam.

"Film starts in one minute. One minute."

With outstretched arms, she rounded up everyone except the children and herded them towards the television set. Petra and husband, Tom, were already side-by-side but disengaged on the sofa. The four in-laws hovered in the wings and watched with appalled expressions while Josie rested her hands on Tom's shoulders. I replaced the card in its envelope and joined Tony by the kitchen door.

"As you all know," Miriam said, "daddy was fond of the movie camera. I have put together a collection of the best clips."

"Do we get the national anthem?" someone asked.

"Quiet in the ranks," Miriam said, and she slipped a DVD into the player.

The compilation began with beaches, sandcastles and silent laughter. I laughed and pointed along with the others at the antics of my father. I even managed to laugh at the realisation that these film clips represented the holidays I had never spent with my dad. It was not the fault of my half-siblings that they could enjoy memories which might have been mine. But I almost stopped laughing when I saw the truth. As a child, I had waited on many occasions for my father to visit. When he had not appeared, I was able to excuse him by telling myself that he had been held up by Black Patch in West Wittering. The reality was that he had been on an anonymous beach or garden and playing with other children.

The clips covered a period that began with prams and beaches and ended with a marriage. What struck me was that, for most of us, the ageing process is imperceptible. But I was forced to watch my father grow old in all but 10 minutes. The last clip showed him on his feet and giving his speech at Tom and Petra's wedding.

"*Alea iacta est*," I heard him say. "For those of you who don't understand Latin, that means: 'the die is cast'." He paused and looked out at the assembled guests with the air of an academic giving a lecture. It looked like my father was expressing feelings of superiority. It was a side of him I had neither seen nor considered.

"A friend of mine thinks everyone should get married because no-one deserves to be happy their entire life, but I hope that you two will prove him wrong and that 50 years from now you will be just as happy and as much in love with each other as you are today."

My father faltered, muttered half words while he

stared over the audience in a way that suggested he had seen a ghost. Pulling himself together, he added:

"Please, don't forget that fortune favours the brave. *'Audentis fortuna iuvat'*."

Miriam leaped forward, took aim with the remote, and my father and the assembled guests disappeared into a pinprick of light on the TV screen. Tom upset the ensuing silence by shrugging off Josie's hands and making for the kitchen. While Petra sobbed, there was a hiss from the kitchen and the click of beer top landing on the floor. Nobody sang the national anthem. I took a step towards Petra but a hand landed on my arm and stopped me in my tracks.

"Don't," said Josie in my ear. "Stay cool. There's nothing you can do."

I was happy to oblige. Part of me knew that by expressing my commiserations, I would be betraying my father.

"Excuse me, everyone."

Heads turned in my direction, and I added:

"I've also got some memorabilia you might want to see."

I reached into my inside pocket and pulled out the paper bag.

When my father went, he left behind his razor and shaving brush, and a paper bag I found in his sock drawer. The bag contained items that became the hooks I employed to hang on to my father after his shadow had faded. Along with his novel, *The White Mountain*, these items enabled me to fantasise and turn my dad into a hero. I made up stories about how he won the war. A spy on a vital mission in Germany, my dad was forced to hide for months in a mountain hut with his blond-haired lover. No wonder he had left us in such a hurry in 1960. The past had caught up with him.

"A few photographs of father in Germany in 1939," I

said. "You may be interested in them."

I stepped over to the dining table and expected the other guests to follow. It had not been my intention to throw the photos down on the table, but my hand struck the chair back, the photos flew from my hand, landed with a slap and spread out star-like beside the New York wreath.

"Whoops," I said by way of apology.

The damage had been done, and the family collectively flinched as if I had slapped their faces. Tony, Josie, Petra and Miriam moved forward and bent over the table like adoring parents over a newborn. Miriam put out her hand and arranged the photos with a light touch of her fingertips. One by one, she drew the photos forward for inspection.

"They show our father on his German trip in 1939," I said, "just a few weeks before the outbreak of war."

The thirteen photos included shots of three men in military uniform, my father and a young man in civilian clothes. There were hotel terraces bathed in the limpid mountain sunlight, and empty beer bottles lined up on tables. In several photos, the presence of a young woman was signalled by an arm draped over the back of a chair. But it was the photo of the bland mountain hut that I found particularly evocative. Most mountain huts I had visited were marked by fluttering flags, hanging flowers and surrounded by people in sturdy boots examining maps and setting compasses. This hut was simply a two-dimensional shape against a backdrop of sky and mountains. There were no people, but my youthful imagination had visited this hut on numerous occasions, and I created my characters. In this hut, father lay low while on the run from units of the German army. For me, it had always been the hut with no people and the hut with no name.

Josie turned the photos over. Three of them had

comments in my father's handwriting. As an adolescent I had read and re-read these comments looking for some secret code that I could decipher. One photograph was annotated with, "Hotel Post, *Oberwald*, August 1939." On the back of another were two words: "Herr H." The man himself had been photographed in the doorway of the Hotel Post and giving a Nazi salute. There was also the shot of the train station in *Oberwald* and the annotation on the back, "So sorry to leave Herr H. When the train pulled away the sky itself was crying. Goodbye N."

Tony slid his fingers underneath one of the photos and let it rest in the palm of one hand. It could have been a piece of valuable pottery but he snapped at me as if I was the family gardener.

"Why didn't you tell us before about these? We had no idea dad was in Germany until we read the obituary."

"I was busy circulating," I said.

"He does look happy," Petra added.

Josie made a noise that sounded like a grunt.

"The appearance of things can be deceptive."

Someone said:

"Do we know who these people are?"

"No idea," I said. "My mother didn't know either. Perhaps some friends he made on his travels."

"Nazis?" Tom said.

He laughed after this remark. It was a cheerful laugh but it sounded wrong. Its discordance threatened the image of my father that I had built up as a child. I stared at him.

"That sort of evil lies in most people," I said. "You, too, are capable of anything. You, too, shouldn't trust yourself."

"Are you calling me a Nazi?" Tom said.

"I'm saying that he, who curses his parents, is also cursing himself."

"He sure ain't my parent, matey."

This exchange was greeted not with a stir but with the silence of people who are confronted by a horrible truth or a nightmare - the recurring dream when your hidden secrets are discovered under your bed.

"By the way," Josie said, "who is the woman?"

"Woman?"

"Yes, here," and she pointed to the bare female arm draped over a chair.

I knew that arm intimately, and my imagination had once attached a head and a beautiful face to it. It was the face that bewitched both my father and his arch enemy and pursuer, Captain Christian Von Stoutenberg and his evil minions. The stage was thus set for epic encounters between father and his rival's men. The climactic scene had my father and Von Stoutenberg in a life-and-death struggle over a waterfall in the Alps while the blond-haired lover looked on. This story was probably inspired by Sherlock Holmes and Moriarty rather than by my childish inventiveness.

"Sorry, I can't help," I said.

"Perhaps he was kind of happy once in his life?"

Josie shuddered and her shoulders stiffened as if in response to a stream of cold air. She remained locked in this position while she clasped her hands and rubbed them together.

"Can we have these?" she asked.

My silence invited them all to stop and stare at me.

"I mean," Josie said, "can you, like, scan them for us and email them?"

The whole family were waiting on my reply as if they were waiting for a judge to hand down a sentence. I kept my expression non-committal for a while. Eventually, I smiled and said:

"Delighted."

"No worries, then."

"The obituary," I said. "Can you send me a copy?"

"I'll scan it and mail it, yeah?"

The film clips and the photographs marked the climax of the post-funeral event, and when I left in the early evening, I thought the door slammed rather too quickly behind me. Alone in the driveway and waiting for my taxi, I scrolled Robby's number and pressed the dial button. While the calling tone buzzed in my ear, I pinched the bridge of my nose between thumb and forefinger. The ringing tone droned on. I was about to press the red button when there was a click and Robby's voice crackled into my ear.

"That you, Pam?"

There was a shuffle from the other end of the connection and the silence which followed had a tense and confrontational quality about it.

"Robby, it's..."

I stumbled, as I usually did, over the next word, but simply acknowledged that I would probably always have an uncomfortable relationship with any word that described the paternal function.

"It's me," I said.

The papers shuffled again and out of the continuing silence came a vision of my son. He was sitting at his desk and working on his latest article. I imagined his head in front of the computer screen; the face pinched and concentrated, the curls on his head a 30-years-younger version of my own.

"I'm back from the funeral," I said.

"How was it, dad?"

I struggled with the disinterested tone of Robby's voice.

"Nice," I said.

"And your lost family?"

Robby sounded like an insurance salesman quizzing a client for personal details. I drummed my fingers on my temple while considering my response, but the tone of Robby's voice was infectious.

"Alright," I said.

"What does 'alright' mean, dad?"

"I was a bit disappointed."

"Why, dad?"

"They did not conform to my expectations."

I knew that I had probably allowed my imagination to dwell on my half-siblings for so many years that what had emerged in my mind was a picture of perfection: the Famous Five children who had absorbed all the paternal love and attention I had missed.

"That's your problem, dad."

"I was amazed that they knew very little about their father's life before he became their father. Can you believe that?"

There was no immediate reply but I heard the sound of Robby's breathing. It came and went in short bursts and eluded interpretation.

"So, what did you know of his life after he left you, dad?"

I held the phone away from my ear and stared at it. There was an edge to Robby's voice that I had never heard before. I then told Robby about the film clips and how indignant I was on hearing my father use Latin to belittle some of the guests.

"It was shocking to see such behaviour," I said.

"He was just human. Is it that old question again? Those terrible words, 'Is this all there is?' Have they returned, dad?"

"Just a minute," I said. "I think that might be the taxi. Hang on a minute."

There was truth in what Robby said. I had always been afflicted with disappointment and an inner voice which nagged me with the question: "Is this all there is?" As a child, holiday destinations had never matched my dreams. As an adult, I suffered from the feeling that whatever I achieved, it was only the shadow of something better. I was well known in my field of history but I saw only the inadequacies in my work. The question, "Is this all there is?" had also led to my unfaithful behaviour and eventual divorce from Robby's mum. When he was old enough, I thought it a good idea to discuss it with him. He now seemed to be throwing it back in my face.

I brought the phone back to my ear.

"False alarm," I said.

"Are you going to see your half-siblings again?"

"I was impressed by two of them."

"Are you going to see them again?"

He took my silence as a negative.

"See, dad? When you married mum, you told me you doubted your ability to be the good husband your imagination had created for you. Are you now doubting your ability to be a good brother, too?"

I shook my head at the phone. Robby was thirty and married, and I thought we had left the years of teenage rebellion behind us. Perhaps the problem was that he and I had been a weekend family and we now needed more time to reconnect.

"Taxi coming," I said. "Give my best to Pam."

There was a harsh intake of breath from the end of the line. Something like a vibration had come with the breath and suggested tension or fear.

"Will do," Robby said and the phone went dead.

The taxi came 10 minutes later.

Driving away to the station, I reflected on the day. Not only was Robby disconnecting from me, I felt that Charles Saddler – the real Charles Saddler - had slipped through the fingers of all of us. What disturbed me most of all was the question, "Is that all there is?" Had it really raised its head again? When Robby's mum left me, I thought I had learned a lesson. By the time I met Liz, I believed myself to be a changed man. Now I was having doubts. The world only changed when we changed. Unless I got a grip, I would do it again. I thought of my wonderful son, Ben, and my wife, Liz, and wondered why I had not yet found the courage to say no to Marie-Claude and another looming affair.

# 4

There is a rustle in the darkness. The man is shifting in his sleep, and the fear of vengeance resurges. He must have put two and two together and seen the truth. My hand finds the table top. I fumble for the book and lift the front cover of *The White Mountain*. The existence of the novel comforts me in these long and dark hours. Its pages flutter against my fingers, and the scent, emanating from the paper, is similar to that given off by a night-blooming flower. It is instantly recognisable. Until recently, this scent would return me to childhood, and I allowed the novel to re-ignite my childish fantasies concerning my father, his blond-haired lover and his fictional struggles with Christian Von Stoutenberg during World War 2.

Since our arrival in *Oberwald* 3 days ago, Josie has helped me ignore the aroma, and I now react to the book in a different way. She has shown me that the text might reflect father's visit here in 1939, and I now read it with the critical eye of an adult. Two days ago, with book in hand, Josie and I climbed the *Kreuzberg*. When we arrived at the bottom of the track that led up to the grave garden, we were like two children unable to wait for Christmas Day. In a shiver of excitement, we stood shoulder to shoulder and read the relevant passages of the book in silence.

*

The road to the Valley of Prisoners rose between two hillocks. As it neared the entrance to the valley, the road gradually became a dirt track. Sergio saw the track winding steeply up the valley like a scar. Above the valley, the two peaks were giant molars with streaks of snow that lay in the crags and reflected the spring sunshine. To his left, the path spiralled up the side of *Monte Croce* and towards the grave garden. To his right, the priest's house stood on top of a hill known as Napoleon's Nose and it was now close above them. Sergio looked with some surprise at the slope of this hill. It seemed so smooth from the village, but in reality, it consisted of tiers that led upwards, one upon the other, until they reached the top. The earth, stirring in its winter sleep, was a glistening green, and the colour was reflected in pools of green light on the shutters of the priest's house. Under the shutters, two large arches gave on to a veranda, from which a wide stone staircase, flanked with Grecian urns, dropped towards a chapel beside the road on which they were walking.

Sergio looked up to the nick in the ridge that marked the top of the valley. From there, the path wound down steeply and disappeared into the forest, which was now a burgeoning green. When the path emerged from the trees, it no longer resembled a scar but was more like an open wound. Alongside the path raced a stream. Plunging and scurrying, it seemed to be saying: "Come with me, but I'll get to the bottom before you."

I clapped the book shut and shook my head.

"There's no bloody chapel here. And there's no house or hill called Napoleon's bloody Nose either."

Josie dismissed my words with a wave of the hand.

"Stay cool, yeah?"

"I am cool."

Josie raised her eyes and met mine head on. Anger was present in the throbbing pulse in her neck and a sneer hovered over her top lip. I spun away from these reactions to my behaviour but there was no escaping from the fact that I was acting like a spoiled child.

"You OK about going on, yeah?"

"Sorry," I said. "I'm just a bit disappointed."

"Why, Nick? Like any other writer, Dad would have used his own experience creatively, yeah? The description of *Monte Croce* had to fit the purpose of the book, get it?"

I flung my hands in the air.

"Got it," I said.

I strode off along the track that led to the grave garden on the *Kreuzberg*. The path cut upwards across lush, green slopes before it joined a mule track. At my back was the sound of rustling grass, falling stones and Josie breathing so closely at my ear she could have been my shadow. Just below the summit, the rustling and breathing ceased. I stamped to a halt and looked over my shoulder. Josie was some metres behind me with her nose in *The White Mountain*. She raised one arm and held it high above her head in the manner of an eager schoolchild.

"Listen to this," she said.

Placing the book in the palm of one hand, Josie resembled a priest about to read from the Holy Scripture.

"Is it worthwhile?" I said. "Will it tell us anything?"

In one crisp movement, Josie brought her fists to her hips and snapped her elbows outwards. The pulse in her neck was throbbing again.

"Sorry," I said.

With a sweeping movement of her arm, Josie brought the book back to reading distance. Her eyes danced over its pages until they locked on to the passage she wanted to read.

"At first," Josie read, "the top of the hill was clearly visible, but when they reached the mule track, the cross disappeared from view."

Josie looked up and fixed questioning eyes on my face.

"That's right, yeah?"

I felt my cheeks redden. Looking around, I assessed the accuracy of the book and tried a genuine smile.

"It was here that Sergio stopped," Josie read. "Unbuttoning his jacket and pulling at the sleeves of his pullover, he looked down on the village. *Quero Vas* lay stark and sharp below them. Sergio was unable to make out any details. Neither the crumbling church wall nor the war memorial beside it were visible."

I scanned the buildings of the town beneath us and watched the cloud shadow running over the roof tops of *Oberwald*. The sunlight flickered on the church tower before the light dimmed and then died. The street lamps appeared to have gone out in the town.

"Could be any place in the mountains," I said and, swinging round, I set off for the summit. The mule track went back and forth through stunted trees and hedges until the cross appeared amongst the trees that lined the crest of the hill. When we arrived on the summit, Josie made directly for the memorial cross. It was placed squarely in the middle of a triangle, and trees had been planted along all three sides. She paused to get her breath before opening the book with a flick of her wrist.

"Sergio felt pangs of disappointment when he saw the cross," she read. "From *Quero Vas*, it was an integral whole and shone like marble in the sunlight. Now he saw how it had been constructed. Nuts and bolts stood out clearly, and the surface seemed patched up with strips of white plastic. It was held to the ground by pieces of rusting wire that reminded Sergio of tent ropes. He felt sorry for the partisans in whose memory the cross had been erected. Somehow Sergio expected more for these people. He felt that they had been let down, their memory cheated."

I concentrated on the ground while a gust of wind moved the branches of the trees. Momentarily, the sunlight shifted and shone on Josie. She had the book close to her chest as if protecting it from harm. At intervals, she looked at the cross and nodded her head.

"It was a moment of stillness," she read, "the light appeared to mellow, and the air of silent things brushed the tips of the long grass. Sergio heard a rustle at his elbow and then, at the push of an invisible hand, the cypress trees began to gently sway."

"Interesting, but...," I began, and then let my words hang in the air. I had intended to infuse my words with optimism but I finished with: "There are no cypress trees here."

I looked down at my hands and, with a slight movement of the shoulders, I said:

"Perhaps we should not expect too much."

Josie's arm sprang out and a finger jabbed at my

chest.

"No," she said. "It's you who should not expect too much."

Her eyes were without criticism and her voice was without anger but she held her hand palm outwards as a signal that told me she required no response. I remained still until Josie lowered her arm, picked up her optimism and allowed it to carry her away again.

"Have you noticed?" she said. "There are two memorials here."

She pointed to an obelisk not 5 metres from the cross. I made my way towards it, and a breeze blew up the valley and reached us on the top of *Kreuzberg*. The wind tugged at my clothes and, when I spoke, a note of optimism had returned to my voice.

"It's to the fallen from World War 1," I said.

"Just a minute," Josie said, thumbing through the pages of the novel.

I waited by the obelisk while thickening clouds curled and rolled and threatened rain.

"Here it is," she said. "This is dad's description of the monument to the fallen of World War 1. It's not on the top of any hill or mountain though. He puts it in the central square of *Quero Vas*. Listen."

She cleared her throat and held the book in front of her.

"There were countless oval sepia prints protected from the elements," she read. "The shiny scrubbed faces were evidence of parental pride. Sergio wondered what their mothers and fathers would have said, had they known, that at the flash of a photographer's bulb, these boys would stare forever outwards at increasingly forgetful generations."

"That could be a description of any war memorial," I said.

"Nick..."

Holding out my hands and lowering my head, I kicked at the ground before raising my arms in a gesture of surrender. I said:

"Ok, got it," and quickly added, "Anyway, it's the memorial to the victims of Fascism that we've come to see, right?"

"Right," Josie said. "Dad's agent said there was something on it we might find kind of interesting."

I stood with bowed head, listening to the sound of my breathing and to my heartbeat. I walked away from the obelisk and joined Josie at the cross. Four faces stared back at ours. They could have been the same faces that looked out at the world from the memorial to the fallen from World War 1. The hair was different, and these prints were clearer, but there was something similar about all these photos of dead heroes and victims. Perhaps it was their youth. I put out my hand, touched one of the prints and let my fingertips run across the engraved names: Anton Beck, Joseph Dreher, Miriam Dornacher and Peter Weil. Under the names was the legend: "Victims of war and tyranny – 16 August 1939." Josie and I backed away from the cross, through the shadow of the trees and out into the flickering sunlight.

Josie muttered something, took a huge intake of breath and covered her mouth with her hands.

"What's up?" I asked.

I detected a note of impatience in my voice, but extravagant behaviour and expansive gestures were things I had come to expect from Josie. Her eyes were like saucers and they were fixed on the cross as though something nasty was emerging from it.

"He was here," she whispered.

I took a step away from her, tilted my head and listened to the moaning hum of the wind in the wires.

"Who was here?"

Josie bit at her bottom lip and shrank away to some

other place.

"Josie?" I said.

She raised her head and looked at me for a while, but her eyes were expressionless.

"Those names," she said.

"What about them?"

"Read them to me."

I moved back into the shade of the trees and leaned towards the cross.

"Anton Beck..."

"No, no," she said, "just the first names."

"Anton, Joseph, Miriam and Peter."

Her expressionless face lit up with sudden comprehension.

"That's it, don't you see?"

"What is 'it' that I don't see?"

"Anthony, Josephine, Miriam and Petra."

Josie's voice drifted away, and I stared in silence at the cross as if wishing it to tell me something. Understanding came with academic detachment. So – these were the names of Josie and her siblings. In *The White Mountain*, the dead people had been partisans. Here on the *Kreuzberg*, they were victims of Fascism. How nice that father had named his children after them.

Josie was frowning at the ground. Her eyelids were screwed up tight as if she was having trouble focusing on something. Eventually, she lifted the book and began reading again.

"Sergio and Beatrice turned together," she read. "Standing in the weakening shadow of the memorial was a figure with a stick. Immobile, solitary and apparently about to blow away in the breeze was old Giovanni. He was silent and still, wrapped in his thoughts until a change came over his expression and he raised his head to the cross. His eyes reflected nothing but emptiness. Sergio guessed they were turned inwards and searching the darkest corners of his memory."

Josie snatched the novel close to her as a fierce gust of wind tossed the book's pages back and forth. She clasped it under her arm and backed away from the cross. The trees around us swayed frantically and the moan in the wires became a high-pitched whine. Then the wind dropped and a fine curtain of rain began to fall. It drew a veil between the hilltop and the rest of the world.

"Cool that we haven't come across an old man called Giovanni and his strange story, yeah?"

"The story about the partisans?" I said. "What was it again? Let me see."

She came and nestled into my shoulder and held the book in front of her. We knew we were both pretending. Unwilling to face our reactions to the names on the cross, we protected ourselves by jumping into Giovanni's story and running ahead of our feelings.

> Giovanni leaned forward on his stick, lifted one hand and pointed an accusing finger.
>
> "Do you think anyone remembers now? And if they do, what do they remember, can you tell me that?"
>
> He did not expect an answer. He raised his stick and indicated the photos on the monument.
>
> "And these faces," he said, "the boys were not even from our town."
>
> "What happened," Beatrice asked gently.
>
> "You will be the first outsiders to hear a story I have wanted to tell for nearly 20 years."
>
> "I know the Germans were not here that night," Sergio said by way of

encouragement.

"Then you know," said Giovanni, "but perhaps you don't know it."

The old man looked down at his hand. Cupped over the walking stick, it was withered and blotchy, and the veins on the back of his hand were as visible as the roots of a tree breaking through the soil. For some time, he muttered to himself while he looked up at the sky and across at the sepia prints. His words, trying to express some deeper thoughts, were fumbling and tentative.

"There are three of them," he began. "They are 18 or 19 years of age. They are going to be heroes. They are going to kill Germans and win the war. They want to be something."

I lifted my head and watched Josie's eyes zigzagging. I heard her vocalise the last five words and she turned the page.

Giovanni hesitated. It seemed to Sergio that the old man's thoughts and memories had been buried for so long they had become petrified.

"We have survived the war. We haven't seen much of it here in *Quero Vas* but we know what can happen to those who harbour terrorists. Whole villages are wiped of the face of the earth. But these youngsters will not listen to reason. They want glory. They want to do their duty. They want to be heroes. We have to lock them up. They are dangerous, you see?"

Giovanni paused and looked searchingly at both Beatrice and Sergio. He seemed disappointed at finding no immediate response and swept at the ground with his stick as if his words had simply expired and now lay at his feet like dead things.

"So," he said, "we put them in a basement until we decide what to do. How can we let them do something so irresponsible? It will be a useless act of violence against an enemy who leave us alone. It will be the end for us. What right do they have to do such a thing?"

Sergio glanced at Beatrice. He wanted to catch her eye and tell her, perhaps, that the old man was not talking to them. He was conversing with his own memories.

"Catya beseeches the villagers to let them go. She begs them. They are just young boys, she says, and one of them is her brother."

Giovanni let his hand gently touch the sepia prints. A tear ran down the old man's cheeks.

"Then one night, five of us go to the basement door. These boys think we have come to release them. They are too young to understand what fear can do. We hear them rising from their basement. They are ready to escape, to be free, to do their duty and become heroes. But we feel nothing. We, too, have our duty, an obligation to our fellows, and we cannot fail them. And their greetings turn to shouts of dismay and then to anger when they hear the door shut with a crash."

There was a long pause as Giovanni gathered himself. After years of imprisonment, his demons were about to break free.

I watched Josie from the corner of an eye. The fine rain had soaked her hair and its ends were curling in tiny ringlets. A drop of rain rolled down her temple as she moved her head from side to side, her brain decoding the written word and deriving meaning. When she came to the end of the page, she turned to the next.

"But what do you think they feel," Giovanni said, "when they hear the rolling metal on concrete?"

He allowed his eyes to flicker from side to side as though searching for an answer. He said:

"Tell me, how long do you think it takes before they realise what the sound is? One second or two, perhaps? Imagine the fear that takes hold of them. What would you feel if you knew you had but moments to live?"

Giovanni had moved away from the monument. He was unwilling to continue while the faces stared out from the past and accused him of such shameful acts.

"I often wonder, Capitano. To hear the sound of grenades rolling on concrete and not to know how long the throwers waited before letting them roll. How long will you have? Two seconds or six? And each second will be a lifetime and each second can mean death."

He hung his head and Sergio tried to

imagine how it must have been for the young men.

"Their screams reach us while we wait for the grenades to explode."

He rested both hands on his stick and his head drooped as if he was falling asleep.

"I hear the screams now when the nights are long and lonely."

He shuddered and his head sank still further until his chin rested on his breast bone.

"They were all blown to pieces, and the bits are taken and we hang them from the lampposts as the Germans would do. It will be an act of warning, and stop such things from happening again."

Giovanni shuddered – perhaps shaking himself free from the demonic remnants that tormented him.

Josie closed the book. The breeze freshened and the trees around us swayed. Mist was now floating in patches over *Oberwald*. I looked at my watch and, catching Josie's eye, indicated that we should leave.

"Appointment in the hotel at 4 o'clock," I said.

We jogged down the hill and, when the path flattened out, we paused.

"We don't need to speak to him now, do we?" Josie asked.

"Him?"

"The hotel manager. We know dad was here, yeah?"

I considered this but I ducked her question by setting off quickly along the path and saying over my shoulder:

"I'd like to know who else was staying in the hotel."

"Nicholas?"

"We could put names to the faces in father's photos,"

I said.

"Nicholas."

The power of this half shout and half scream forced me to stop dead in my tracks and turn to face her.

"He must have known them," Josie said, indicating the *Kreuzberg* with a hitchhiker's movement of the thumb.

"The victims, you mean? Maybe."

"Not 'maybe', Nicholas. He must have known them."

"Otherwise, why did father give you and your siblings their names, is that it?"

"It makes me feel kind of responsible, yeah."

"Responsible for what?"

She turned and lifted her face to the summit cross.

"We carry their names, yeah? And you too, you..."

"We're not responsible for anything," I said.

I had intended to sound sympathetic, interested and caring. Instead, my tone had been sharp and dismissive and it sent Josie hurrying on towards town. I watched her for a while and wondered why I was punishing her. The light rain had stopped, and I raised my head to assess the sky before stumbling off behind her. I managed to close the distance between us to around 10 metres when she span round.

"Come on, Nick. What's up?"

"Nothing."

"Yeah, right. Like - have you seen your face?"

"I don't have a mirror."

"Very funny."

"What's the matter with my face?"

"Since we arrived on the summit, it's been, like, as dark as thunder."

Without waiting for a reply, Josie turned and sped down the track and towards the road. I set off in pursuit.

By now, we were on the edge of town. The fact was that her comment about my unrealistic expectations had touched on a sore nerve. My son, Robby, had already exposed this nerve when we met in London just a few days previously. He seemed to take delight in suggesting that it was my father' absence that had affected me most. This absence had enabled me to develop the fantasy of the perfect father. This had turned into a need for the perfect woman. But it had not stopped there. Anything that did not match the perfection of my expectations was flawed and unworthy of consideration. I quickened my step. Josie deserved better from her half-brother. I owed her an explanation and an apology. I was about to call out to her when there was a voice from behind.

"Is this yours?"

# 5

Were it light in the hut, I would open *The White Mountain* and scan its pages for more clues that the story parallels father's activities in *Oberwald* in 1939. But silent darkness surrounds us, and I suppose everything outside is covered in snow. I think I hear it crackling while it settles.

*The White Mountain* plays out in the Dolomite village of *Quero Vas*. Lying astride the old road that crosses the mountains between *Rovereto* and *Vicenza*, the village has been cast adrift by the building of the motorway, and the people of *Quero Vas* are now simply living out their history. The natural beauty of the area attracts walkers. Some arrive in the village to visit the monument to the fallen from World War 1. Others come to the memorial on the summit of *Monte Croce* and stand in silent remembrance of the young partisans killed during World War 2.

The novel begins with the arrival of two Neapolitans in *Quero Vas*. The outsiders are Luca and his beautiful daughter, Beatrice, and their intention to establish a walkers' hut in the mountains brings them into conflict with Gustavo Spilimbergo. Nicknamed "The German," Spilimbergo has run the official refuge for years. The ensuing tension soon involves Sergio Fracassini, Captain of Carabinieri and the only policeman in the area. His investigations reveal that *Quero Vas* harbours a terrible secret - the villagers themselves were responsible for the murder of the partisans memorialised on the hill. Sergio also learns that the villagers will take any measures to cover up their past crimes. These measures include the removal of their policeman and the inquisitive newcomers from the south of Italy.

Reading the book has reawakened, in both Josie and I, a sense of our father and the recurring themes that permeate his works. We wonder whether his own experience determined his obsession with the power of evil, with rough justice and with prejudice against minorities. It is also possible, as Robby pointed out when we met in London a few days ago, that father was simply a product of a post-war era that rejected Fascism and all it stood for.

We have no solid evidence that the book is autobiographical, but I now believe that the comments made by Peter Germaine, father's former literary agent, were correct. He suggested that we might find traces of the novel's *Monte Croce* on the *Kreuzberg*, and we did. His claim that what happened in *Oberwald* in 1939 influenced everything father wrote may well be true. What concerns me now is Germaine's assertion that the writing of *The White Mountain* was a purging experience for its author. Since last night, I can hazard a guess at what father felt he needed to atone for. I have no idea how much the other man in the hut knows and nor do I know what he will do about it.

*

About a week after the funeral, I received the first of many emails from Josie. She had written it in the morning but I always dealt with my private mails in the evening. Most of our early email exchanges could have been written by people living in different time zones.

Nicholas
Cool to meet you last week and loved the photographs you showed us. They were a revelation. Why was dad in Germany so close to the outbreak of war? Did your mother tell you? Did he talk about it? Never mentioned it to me. You know things about his life before 1960, and I know a bit about his life after that. Dad never talked to me about anything. He said once that the young never listen to the old. Like so much of his life, he clearly decided to take control of everything by not discussing his past at all. His childhood and upbringing were no-go areas. Some of the details in his obit were news to all of us. Weird!

I am helping Miriam clear out the house before she puts it on the market. Dirty business trawling through dad's stuff. Every item had associations for him but most of it is junk to us. It's soooooooooo uncool to see your father's life packed into plastic bags and left in the rain for collection by the bin men.

His office is something else. This holy of holies contains THE writing desk and THE bookcase. There are boxes full of stuff that dad wanted to keep close. We clear it out in short doses. You get a glimpse into his mind and we feel like intruders.

Btw, I have been looking at *The White Mountain* again. The dedication reads: "To N with much love." Now that dad is dead, this N seems to be springing up everywhere – in books and on cards accompanying strange wreaths from New York. Dad must have been in love with her. How cool is that? Skimming through the book, I was struck by Sergio's meeting with Spilimbergo in the mountains. Do you know the bit? These monstrous individuals often appear in his work. Do you think Spilimbergo was someone dad knew?

Can we meet up again soon? Would be soooo cool to know you better. I still have the urn. Dad is controlling us from beyond! Lol!!! He says his ashes must be scattered on the *Widderstein* and he is telling us when! Can you believe that? It's the 23rd August.

Really look forward to getting the scanned photos. Must dash.

Love
Josie

Josie's candid mail was in such contrast to the frigid formality of official university mails that I laughed aloud. Its adolescent and direct style reminded me of the mails I received from some students but Josie's mail was laced with adult seriousness and consistent with the split personality I had met at the funeral. Still chuckling, I got up from my desk and made directly for my bookcase. My arm was already outstretched and reaching for the volume with the white dust jacket; top shelf, and fifth from the left. My index finger landed on the spine and paused above the book's name, *The White Mountain*, and its author, Charles Saddler.

I pulled the book from the case and let it rest in the clutch of my hand. I swung the front cover open with my thumb and stroked the pages with my fingertips until I reached the one I wanted. I squeezed the paper between thumb and forefinger and blinked at the dedication: "To N with much love." I must have skimmed over these words a hundred times but my eyes had not, until that moment, lingered long enough to invest the words with sense or meaning.

I leafed through the book until I found the passage Josie had mentioned in her mail. I was soon carried away by the familiar narrative, and the paragraphs unfolded with their tale of harassment and fear and peopled by characters as alive as only a child could make them.

Sergio had been investigating complaints about a reclusive old lady, Caterina Bertone, and her cats. These investigations provided the policeman with information on the partisans and their memorial on *Monte Croce*. Sergio eventually broke into Caterina's house and found a "protrusion from behind the sofa." He was shocked to understand that the old lady had been dead for some time and half-eaten by her cats.

At the time of its publication, the book's focus on alienation and prejudice was very much in tune with other novels and films of the period. Even so, its gritty realism caused a stir in the early sixties. When I was very young, none of this mattered to me in the least. The book and the photos I had found in the sock drawer simply provided me with access to my father and the possibility of finding the presence of two words: "Black" and "Patch." When I was old enough to understand the description of the old lady's cadaver and the eye, hanging loosely from its socket, shining and moist and staring at him, it haunted me for years.

In the novel, this gruesome discovery caused Sergio to go into a state of shock. Finding nobody to help him, Sergio decided to take himself away from the village.

He walked quickly, desperately trying to keep ahead of a cloud of insensibility that was gathering behind him and threatening to suck out his energy. He rushed through the forest, jogged along the stream and up the Valley of Prisoners until he reached the nick where the valley joined the ridge. Breathless, Sergio sat down, crossed his legs, and tried to find some peace. Then, he thought he heard someone calling out to him.

He looked down upon the browns and greens of the forest. They were fading away, as colours will do in the light of late afternoon, and the tree tops were swaying in a light wind. He looked beyond the forest and at the hills that weighed low and darkly on the horizon. In his disturbed state, Sergio wondered if the mountains themselves had whispered to him.

Sergio pushed himself up from the ground. He shook his head and rubbed his eyes, but he knew that the struggle was lost. The cloud of insensibility had followed him up the mountain and now enveloped him. For a moment, he felt he was moving out of time. The sun had disappeared behind an archway of clouds, and below the arch, the trees swayed to a quickening wind. At that moment, Sergio felt a presence behind him.

The person was unseen but tangible, a stirring in the air of someone who had come and who had yet to pass. Spinning round, Sergio saw a figure. Its outline was blurred in the gathering twilight, but taking shape as it neared. The figure appeared to be creeping up from behind until, just short of him, it stopped.

It was then that he recognised Spilimbergo. The German was flustered and sweating profusely. He swung his muscular arm upwards and held it there, hovering above him, his fingers wrapped round a large stone.

"He's going to kill me," Sergio thought.

I hesitated and pulled myself out of the story. I was disturbed to realise that, for me, Spilimbergo was still one of Von Stoutenberg's minions and another of the enemies my father had to deal with while lying low in the mountains with his blond lover. In other words, although I was no longer a child, I was reading with the mind of one.

The problem was that, as a youngster, I had skimmed these pages countless times in my attempts to reach my father. By the age of twelve, I understood most of the words. By my early teens, I knew the layout of the book intimately and I even recognised the major themes that dominated father's work. Unfortunately, my developing understanding of the book stopped at that point. This was probably due to the usual distractions of growing up and, by the time I reached 16 years of age, the book remained largely untouched on the bookshelf. The consequences were that, even after a gap of more than 40 years, my 58-year-old eyes were skimming the pages, but it was the child in me who interpreted the text.

A raging anger that his life was to be

snatched from him almost woke Sergio to the imminent threat, but he was unable to move. Suddenly, Spilimbergo's face was pressed closely to his.

"No, not yet," he said. "I have more important people to deal with."

The German's force of expression barely touched Sergio. Rooted to the spot, he felt himself to be untouchable and far above the commonality of human emotion. Spilimbergo let the stone fall from his hand, lowered his arm, and his fingers gripped the policeman's shoulder.

"But I'll come back for you, Fracassini. You can count on it."

Spilimbergo brushed against Sergio's elbow, but before he could take one step further, Sergio put out his hand and touched him on the shoulder.

"Just a minute," he said.

His voice sounded strange to him, and he heard himself ask, "Who is it you are talking about? Who is it you have to deal with?"

As I read, time slid by and only when I heard the church clock chiming midnight did I look up from the book. Josie's question concerning the identity of "The German" was forcing me to forget Von Stoutenberg and to find new images and details in the book. I was beginning to see Spilimbergo from a different angle. Did "The German" have his origins in father's imagination or was he the ghost of someone father once knew? Perhaps he was the product of a variety of people known to my father and flung together with some imagination to produce an individual. Now that father was no longer with us, we could not ask him. Perhaps, we would never be able to discriminate between fact and fiction.

Spilimbergo let out an explosive oath and, spinning round, he raised his arm. In a state of near paralysis, Sergio was unprepared for the swinging hand. He was vaguely looking for the stone when there was a sound like an explosion in his head, a vivid orange flame in front of his eyes, and pain struck the side of his face. Sergio fell sideway and rolled over. He found himself lying on his back in perfect silence. Then, out of the silence came an excited and gleeful chuckle.

"An eye for an eye and perhaps a tooth for a tooth, Fracassini, eh?"

Sergio picked himself up, staggered forward and then remained still. He shook his head. His burning cheek and the trickle of blood running down his chin woke Sergio from his inertia and filled him with a sense of cold purpose. A fine spray, thrown up by the stream, was drifting in the air and catching the last rays of the sun. For a moment, Sergio watched Spilimbergo plunging through the fine curtain of dispersed light. Then, with an absence of emotion, Sergio set off in pursuit.

Closing the book, I clicked on to Josie's mail and then hit the reply button. Twenty minutes later, I typed out my message.

Dear Josie
I have scanned the photos you want and

they are attached. You can blow them up. Some of them look nice like that. They certainly reveal things I haven't noticed before. The girl's upper arm now has a curl of very light blond hair resting on it. The ashtrays and beer mats are clearly marked as belonging to the Hotel Post, *Oberwald*.

But the one that really fascinates me is that one that shows father laughing. The enlarged version shows something I have not noticed before. He is wearing a flower on his lapel just over his heart. I am not certain but it looks like edelweiss. Another lies on the table but it could belong to anyone.

I've just re-read the passage you mention from *The White Mountain*. If Spilimbergo, aka "The German," was based on someone father knew, it would be news to me! The dedication is interesting. How I wish it would come alive and speak to us. Yes, N is turning up everywhere. She is on the reverse side of my photo of *Oberwald* station, remember? "So sorry to leave Herr H. When the train pulled away, the sky itself was crying. Goodbye N."

N belongs to that period of father's life that you call the dark and long silence. I am inclined to see it as distance. 1939 and N belong to a place so far away that most, if not all, connections with it are broken. The only way into this territory is by way of old photos, the content of his writings and odds and ends that turn up with wreaths from New York. The books pose questions of their own. How much of himself did father put into them?

By the way, I very much look forward to getting the *obit*. Do we know who wrote it?

Why don't you come and visit us in Southsea? We'd love to see you, and Ben is looking forward to meeting his one and only aunt.

Yours sincerely
Nicholas.


The last paragraph was written at the insistence of my wife, Liz. She had been badgering me about it since I came back from the cremation. In her eyes, meeting someone who belonged to me was the opportunity of a lifetime. I think Liz saw me as an enigma – someone who, seemingly, had no connections to anyone else. "You're a lost soul," she often said, "wandering through life with no luggage."

By the time I'd finished with my other private mails, I was surprised to see a message from Josie in my in-box.


Nicholas

I have something sooooo cool to tell you. First tnx for the scans and the invite. I'd love to come to Southsea. What about the beginning of next month – say 6 June? Does that work? Btw, I think the flower on dad's lapel is edelweiss. This symbol of courage, purity and love (as Miriam put it) seems to be springing out of the dark and long silence and surprising us all. It even falls out of envelopes accompanying wreaths!

Now for my new find. N has turned up yet again! Miriam and I found her in dad's office this afternoon. Actually, we found two things. The first is a box, and in the box is an empty casket containing a small card. The card has another poem on one side. On the other side is the inscription: "To CS with love from N. August 1939." Did your mother ever mention a former lover? What the casket contained is a mystery.

I'll bring these with me when we meet. It'll be really cool to meet you and a real family.

We also found the sketch of a short story. It is unfinished and certainly unpublished. I'll bring it when I come.

Must dash

Love

Josie

P.S. Attached is the obit. It's from *The West Country Gazette*. I rang the paper and they said it was written by dad's old publisher.

Dear Josie

That's great. Saturday 6 June would be good for us too. Look forward to seeing you and the new finds then. Now, I'm off to read the obit.

Sincerely

Nicholas

But there was another mail in my inbox and I needed to deal with it. It was a message from Marie-Claude entitled: "Are you attending the conference in Brighton?" I opened the mail and clicked the reply button. My hand hovered over the keyboard for some time before I logged out without replying. Then, I downloaded Josie's attachment and printed it out.

## Charles Saddler obituary

In a writing career that spanned four decades, Charles Saddler, who has died aged ninety, published six crime novels and two collections of short stories. He was also a book reviewer for *The Exeter Magazine*.

A Devon resident, Saddler made his name with his novel, *The White Mountain* (1962). His later books never matched the commercial success of his first, and, typically, he blamed himself and the melancholia that laced his writings. Other factors were also at work. His fiction was based on the post-war belief in the fairness and incorruptibility of British justice and the assurance that evil-doers would inevitably get their just deserts. These core beliefs were widely held in the 1940s and 1950s but began to disintegrate in the 1960s, and Saddler's books lost their appeal.

Saddler was born in India where his father had a career in the Indian army. Aged eight, Saddler was packed off to school in England. During the holidays, he was cared for by a woman named Mrs Wandsworth. The poor treatment and neglect he experienced until he reached the age of twelve may have influenced his writing, in particular his sympathy with the powerless.

A spell at a boarding school, the United Services Institute, provided Saddler with a degree of stability. He excelled in outdoor sports and was a crack shot. For 2 years, he represented the OTC at the public schools shooting championships in Bisley.

In 1938, he was offered a place at Jesus College Oxford. Often a man ahead of his time, Saddler decided to put Oxford off and take what was, essentially, a gap year. In August 1939, he found himself in Germany and, with war imminent, he returned to England. In February 1942, both his parents were killed during the Japanese invasion of Singapore. Saddler seems to have been emotionally detached from the event. In a BBC Radio Devon interview given in 1970, he said of his father: "As to my early years, I regret not realising sooner that I lived in my father's shadow. It seems hardly fair that a man I barely knew should have had such an influence on my life."

On the outbreak of war, Saddler became a pacifist and pleaded conscientious objection. Sent to work on a farm in Sussex, he began writing his first novel, *The White Mountain*, but it was nearly 20 years before the book was completed. This story of crime and cover-up also reflects the loneliness of existence and deals with the figure of the stranger in our midst and the reactions of people to others who are somehow different. These themes infuse all his major works: *The Dividing Line* (1956), *The Forest* (1960), *Worth the Candle* (1970), *The Distance of Memory* (1981) and his last novel, *Lilly* (1989).

With the war over, Saddler decided to put off Oxford indefinitely and he concentrated on writing. Settling in London, he soon found the writing life hardly gave him enough to live on and, in 1949, he took a job with the British Council in Verona, Italy. He made many friendships with visiting writers, and this proved an advantage when he returned to England in 1959. He became president of the Crime Writers Association in 1963. Although his books never sold in huge numbers, he seemed to make enough money to give up other work altogether and focus on his writing. In 1991, he bought a house in Ottermouth and lived there with his eldest daughter, Miriam, until his death.

Saddler was a great traveller, and much of his fiction was set outside Britain. This made him a real cosmopolitan writer. His international outlook is, perhaps, most clearly reflected in his two volumes of short stories, *Postcards* and *Is that all there is?* His youthful passion for climbing and mountains is also reflected in such stories as "Edelweiss" and "A Place I Fear to Tread."

In 1991, he inherited a considerable sum of money. He always claimed that his subsequent decision to stop writing was based on the fact that he had nothing more to say. Aged seventy-two, he took a part-time position with *The Exeter Magazine.* In an interview given on the occasion of his eighty-fifth birthday in 2005, Saddler said: "I had some moments in life – moments that were truly worth living for. And I have written one or two good books. Apart from that, what is all the fuss about?"

He is survived by one son from his first

marriage, by a son and three daughters from
the second and by six grandchildren.

This public obituary told me many facts about my
father's life that I had never known and was, as Josie
described, weird. I crept out of my office and tiptoed
down the corridor to the sound of Liz's light snoring.
Peeking into Ben's bedroom, I saw his silhouette
sprawling in a fling of arms and legs. In the bathroom, I
opened the cabinet over the sink and drew out the
shaving brush. I stroked its bristles over my cheeks, my
chin and my neck and replaced it in its cup. This shaving
brush and the razor were amongst the few personal items
father left behind in 1960. When I was a child, it never
occurred to me to ask my mother why she kept these
items. But these tools, designed for a manly and polished
appearance, were now in my bathroom cabinet. I saw
them every day, retired at a casual angle in his shaving
cup. In contrast to the obituary, they were a private
memory of my father and they belonged to nobody else
but me.

# 6

I know that the hours of darkness are ending. Light is creeping through the window, and I tiptoe towards it, with the novel in hand, to greet the returning world. But there is fog and, while I watch it curling around the crags outside, the sound of a voice appears in my head. The voice belongs to father's former literary agent, and his words will not go away. "It's all in *The White Mountain*. It was a purging experience."

The voice fades when the mountains reveal themselves as silhouettes in the sky. Silence hangs there while the rising world holds its breath.

Josie and I certainly found similarities between *The White Mountain's Monte Croce* and *Oberwald's Kreuzberg* when we visited it 2 days ago. But my academic background compels me to admit that there is no evidence to suggest that these similarities are anything other than coincidence. Similarly, the agent's claim that the unfinished piece was the last chapter of a story which began in 1939 cannot be proved.

What I am sure about is that Josie and I are tapping into the past. We were once disconnected from the comments written on father's *Oberwald* photos. The string of letters that made up the words "Hotel Post," "Herr H" or "The sky was crying" were scribbles on a white background. Over the past months, these phrases have developed their own associations for Josie and me. They are now connected with family, love and death. The same is true of the names engraved on the *Kreuzberg* memorial. Only 2 days have passed since we saw these names but they are now associated with murder and cover-up.

Through these new connections, we can feel the distance of time and it occasionally reverberates in the present. The riot in *Oberwald* 2 days ago was one such shock and reminded us that however much some people might want to forget it, the past never goes away.

The silence around me is disturbed only by the drip-dripping on the tarpaulin and the breathing of my companions. The fog rises, and the mountains disappear from view. This fog could so easily be the same fog that surrounded us that day last June when Josie came to visit us.

*

Although we were expecting her, we missed the first ring of the doorbell. It must have been drowned out by a blast from the foghorn, which had been sounding since daybreak from the harbour entrance. Several weeks had passed since the cremation, but my imagination had transformed my half-sibling into a slightly flawed individual. A woman, I said to Liz, who flirted with married men at her father's funeral was clearly frivolous. Liz raised an eyebrow and gave me a look that suggested she knew something I did not.

"We have no right," she said, "to judge anyone. Nor is it wise to expect anything from them."

Liz opened the front door to a variation of my imaginative creation. The ball of black hair was now tinged with red and had a frizzy, crazy look that was more suited to a punk-inspired party than a family household. Liz was not in the least bit fazed. She grabbed Josie by the arm, stepped around me, and guided her into the sitting-room.

They settled themselves on opposite ends of the sofa and immediately got down to the nitty-gritty – in other words, relationships. The ladies were a perfect fit and, for much of that afternoon, I might just as well not have been there. I was one of several people referred to as "he." I watched them from the kitchen while I made the tea, and Ben made paper planes on the lounge table.

After much deliberation, Liz had adopted what she called her "casual, legal-consultant look." This consisted of a conservative skirt and blouse and it matched the active-listening skills which she had acquired on a course and which she practised with her clients at work. Throughout the afternoon, Liz kept her hands together, maintained eye contact, and made the appropriate sounds and encouraging nods while, at all times, keeping an ear turned towards her interlocutor.

Josie was aflame in an orange and red dress. Watching her from the kitchen, it was clear that, for Josie, speech and gestures were tightly connected. Her hands performed a dance. Sometimes graceful and sometimes crude, her gestures punctuated and underlined her words. She seemed to throw these from her mouth with assertive nods of her head until the eyes and arms retreated and, lifting her chin, she sat back against the cushions and challenged Liz to disagree.

Occasionally, their raised voices drifted into the kitchen with the drones of the foghorn.

"He used to stay away for days at a time," Josie said.

"And why do you think he did this? No, no glue on

the table, Ben dear."

"I could never, like, depend on him..."

"And how did your mother deal with it? What a pity she died so young. Breast cancer you say? Yes, do show us how it flies, dear."

"All he could say was that we had screwed up our lives."

"No, no buts, Ben; please take it outside into the garden... Screwed up your lives? And how did you feel about that?"

"I was outraged. What a dumb comment. Screwing up your life is life, isn't it?"

"Maybe it is, but how did you feel, dear?"

"How would any woman feel?"

"Rejected?"

"Rejected is a loaded word," Josie said.

"Yes, it is, isn't it? And what did you do about these feelings?"

"Behaved badly to get his attention."

"And what do you think his problem was?"

"Kind of depends who's defining the word 'problem', yeah?"

As the afternoon wore on, so the touching started. It began with finger brushes of the forearm and ended with a firm clasping of hands and both women on the brink of tears. When Josie went into the garden for a cigarette, Liz said to me:

"She's 38 years old and unmarried. The sad thing is that she'd like a committed relationship but she doesn't know how go about it. That makes her afraid. The rest is all a cover-up."

"How do you know all that?"

"No need to look so bemused," Liz said.

"But did she tell you this?"

"Of course not," Liz said with a smile.

Josie certainly did not conform to my memories of

the in-your-face woman from the funeral reception. Living inside her was another person, one, perhaps, I had glimpsed in her very first email to me. This person was sensitive and unafraid to share what she felt when forced to pack up her father's belongings and leave them for the bin men.

"Maybe she's just insecure," I said.

"Don't give me that disapproving look," Liz said. "We're not all as perfect as you might like, dear. If she has relationships with married men, as you claim, it's because she knows they cannot commit. This makes her feel safe. She's a magazine editor, by the way, did she tell you?"

"Should I be impressed?" I said. "What's a magazine editor, after all? Someone who works with words but who doesn't write herself?"

"Depends on your perspective, dear. What would you say to someone who described you, the historian, as a person who lives in the past and can't deal with the present?"

I mustered as much nonchalance as I could, but before I uttered a word, the foghorn emitted a deep blast and Josie strode back into the room.

"Did you want to say something, dear?" Liz said to me.

I shook my head. Nonchalance was not something that could be repeated. While Liz bundled Ben into the adjacent television room, Josie pulled a jewellery casket from her bag. She put the casket on the table while a fanfare of trumpets announced the beginning of Ben's film.

The casket was about 3 inches by 3 inches and the top was vaulted. I saw no maker marks but the front had a thin outline of the German cross embossed in silver. I picked the casket up. It had a round push-button closure which invited me to open it.

"This is the item we found in dad's office, yeah? The one I emailed you about?"

Liz came back into the room with the drone of the foghorn. She nestled into my shoulder as the lid of the casket sprang open. I picked the card out and scanned its text.

"To CS with love from N. August 1939."

I flicked the card over. It read:

"The end of the affair will be your departure. It is a dream I will dream all my life."

I gave the card to Liz and muttered the inscription to myself while laser guns squealed from the television room.

"What do you make of it?" I said.

"It's cool," said Josie.

"Why don't you just tell us where it comes from, dear?"

"The *Rubaiyat* of Omar Khayyam."

I looked at Liz and Josie but their faces revealed nothing.

"You know," I said, "the Persian poet and astronomer."

Liz raised her eyebrows and both she and Josie tightened their crossed legs while restrained laughter rippled through their cheeks and into their eyes.

"What is the problem?" I asked.

My innocent question tipped Liz and Josie over the edge.

"Do take off your academic clothes," Liz said into the palm of her hand. The ensuing laughter was contagious and it bound the three of us together. We rocked back and forth like children but I could not help thinking that, had I been unable to hear, I might have thought Josie was crying. Our laughter faded, first to chuckles, and then to the occasional sigh. When all that remained were light smiles on our faces, I said:

"You remember the wreath, don't you, Josie?

"The thing from the long and dark silence, yeah?"

"Yeah, and it came with edelweiss and a photo, didn't it? And there was a dedication and some lines of poetry on the back of the photo, right?"

"Right. The dedication read 'To N with love from CS, August 1939'," Josie said. "Underneath, there was something about being happy now and not living on wind."

"Exactly. Those lines are also from the *Rubaiyat,* if I'm not mistaken."

I excused myself, went to my office and googled the words, "happy" and "live on wind." I was back in the room a few minutes later and charged with my findings. Liz and Josie were poring over some sheets of foolscap that were scattered between them on the sofa. Words and smiles passed between them. From the next room came the whoosh-whooshing sounds of Ben fighting an imaginary foe.

"You need to read this," Liz said, gathering up the foolscap pages and offering them to me.

I held up the palm of my hand.

"Listen," I said.

I paused in order to dramatise what I was going to tell them, but neither Josie nor Liz was on the edge of their seats and Liz irritated me further by shuffling the bundle of papers in her hand. I eventually opened my mouth to speak but at that moment the foghorn let out a drone that sounded like a warning.

"The Gods have intervened," Liz said and, holding the pages under my nose, she added, "You really should read this."

"What is 'this' that can't wait until tomorrow?"

"It's a kind of sketch for a short story," Josie said. "We found it in the bookcase in his office. The 1991 date suggests he must have started it at the very end of his writing career. It might explain why he asked for his ashes to be scattered in *Oberwald*. Cool, yeah?"

"It?"

"Like, dad's relationship with N."

She clasped her hands together and the flat tone with which Josie uttered these last words suggested to me that she had only a slender hold over her feelings. The threat of an emotional display needed countering with some academic distance.

"Let's look at what we know. The story..."

"Men can be so slow," Liz said.

"Dad's relationship with N was not like a passing passion, Nicholas."

"You're missing the point," I said.

"What is the point, dear?"

"The point is," I said, "we've no evidence."

"This was a lifelong commitment," Josie said. "It must've been really cool for him."

Ben then appeared in the doorway. He was on the brink of tears.

"He's going to fight his daddy."

"It's only a film, dear."

"Can God stop it?"

"Stop what, dear?"

"He's going to fight his daddy."

Ben was genuinely upset, and Liz got up to comfort him. Josie still had her hands locked together but her arms and shoulders were trembling as if from cold. She lowered her head, unclasped her hands and stared at her open palms as though in wonder at some rare species of insect she was holding. Another burst of music suggested Ben had settled down to a film, and Liz came back into the room.

"Are you ready for this?" she said, holding up the bundle of papers and placing it in my outstretched hand.

Josie pulled out a packet of cigarettes and a lighter,

and she and Liz headed towards the garden door. I heard Josie say:

"It might well be the last thing he wrote. Strange but the story stops..."

I was no longer listening. I recognised the neat, right-slanted writing immediately. The text was marked with numerous corrections and notes, but the thrust of this, the last story, was clear.

As far back as he could remember he had been like this. Even when he had still been a writer, he would put off the moment of starting. And so, it was now. He had written the note. The bottle of pills was open beside the whisky, and he had locked the door. Still, he paced around the room, sometimes supporting his broken body on chairs or tables.

The pain was getting worse. He was a penniless arthritic, written out, and of no use to anyone. It was right that he should end his own life. The qualities that had made him a successful writer had left him friendless and lonely.

There was a knock on the door.

"Mr Barnes, sir. Mr Barnes."

It was the porter.

"Are you at home, sir?"

Damn the man's eyes. Not now. Why couldn't he leave an old man alone to die in peace?

"There's a letter for you, sir."

Three flights of stairs were nothing to the porter, but the youngster knew how difficult they were for the cantankerous old man who lived on the top floor. The porter was persistent.

"Looks important, sir."

"Slip it under the door," growled Nigel Barnes, "and leave me."

There was a pause, and then the corner of an envelope appeared on the doormat.

"Maybe an old flame, sir."

The young porter was attempting a joke; a flame to brighten Nigel's day. Nigel made no response. He listened to the sound of footsteps clattering down the stairs. When the clattering stopped, Nigel snatched up the letter.

An old flame? No chance of that, Nigel thought. He tossed the envelope onto the table and beside the bottle of pills. There had not been many women in his life. Writing had been an all-consuming passion, and his existence had been self-centred. He had been married - twice - but both his wives had left him years ago. And before that? Maybe just once, the summer of 1939, there had been an earnest youth, a young German Jewess and the burning Italian sun. They had escaped the torrid Venetian heat and met at the bicycle-hire shop on the Lido. They rode along the seafront to the end of the island where they waited for the boat for *Pellestrina*.

Lying in the shade of a cypress tree, he had told her of his burning ambition. "To become a writer, and to be famous and respected."

She encouraged his grand ideas, sympathised with his passion and his desire. Nigel felt her misery when she told him of her wretched life, of what it meant to be a Jewess in Germany. What she wanted was to escape prejudice, hatred and oppression and to know freedom. He understood her then and he recalled the compassion he had felt now. He recalled it with such intensity that he gasped. The feeling was in such stark contrast to the barren intellectual life he had led.

He grabbed at the letter, tore it open and shook the contents onto his lap. There were two enclosures. One had an American stamp on it and was addressed to him in neat handwriting. The other was from a company of London solicitors. What did they want now? Didn't they ever stop demanding money? Nigel chuckled. There was nothing he could give now.

He closed his eyes and felt again the compassion and the heat of the sunlight on the Venetian lagoon. How they had laughed and talked together. *Pellestrina*, the trattoria, sitting on the terrace in the stillness of the afternoon sun; yellow plaster walls, soft red roofs, green shutters closed to the sunlight, Corvo wine, the fishing boats and the hazy blue silhouette of Venice across the water.

He knew she had felt those moments too. They were like a thread making sense of their lives. Barely adult, they were no longer children, but they were at a crossroads and they seized the present.

They took the last boat across the lagoon, and in the morning, she said: "Please, I want that I have something to remember you, Nigel Barnes, my writer." And then she added: "Write me something that will stay by me all my life."

He had taken a postcard from his pocket, turned it over and written something inspired by the *Rubaiyat* of Omar Khayyam on the back of it.

"And I shall forever be your inspiration," she said.

He never saw her again. She went back to Germany and, two weeks later, the war broke out. He supposed she were dead.

Nigel opened his eyes. Outside it was pouring down. He sliced open the letter from the solicitors.

It concerned the last will and testament of a Mrs Patterson, now deceased, of Jacksonville Carolina. It appeared that the late Mrs Patterson had named him as the recipient of the larger part of her fortune. Nigel blinked. There must be some mistake. He had never known anyone by the name of Patterson. He muttered angrily at this disturbance. They were going to hound him to the grave; well, so be it.

Mrs Patterson, the letter went on, had married wealthy art dealer Rudi Patterson. On his death, his wealth had passed to her but on her death in a road accident several months earlier and having no family of her own, Mrs Patterson had left almost everything to Nigel. He was urged to telephone Klein Cohen and partners as soon as possible. Klein Cohen had also been instructed to pass on a letter from Mrs Patterson to Mr Barnes and the epistle was enclosed therein.

Nigel leaned forward painfully and picked up the envelope. He did not recognise the handwriting. This must be a cruel joke. Had he offended someone so much that they should want to play such a trick? Maybe it was a fan; or maybe just a case of mistaken identity. He had never been to America, he had never known many Americans and, as far as he knew, his books had never been popular there.

Nigel pushed his finger under the sticky flap and ripped it open Slipping his hand inside, he slid out a postcard. There were just a few words on one side of it, the second half of a sentence:

"And in the track of a hundred thousand years out of the heart of dust, hope sprang again – like greenness."

It was the *Rubaiyat* and it...

I turned the paper around a few times.

"Yes," said Josie. "It's unfinished."

She and Liz were standing at the terrace doors.

"In the middle of a sentence?" I said.

Josie smiled.

"The end of something, whether it be life itself or a career, cannot always be planned down to the last detail, yeah?"

"For God's sake..."

"Don't look so shocked, dear," Liz said.

I slapped at the pages with the back of my hand.

"Look," I said, shaking the story in the air. "It shocks me that the protagonist, Nigel Barnes, writes some lines from the *Rubaiyat* on the back of a postcard and this postcard turns up years later."

"What's to shock? It's cool. Mirrors reality, yeah?"

I looked through the glass of the terrace doors and into the garden, and considered the extent to which any fiction reflects the life of its author.

"So, you think father was writing about his own experiences?"

Josie breathed deeply through her nose, lifted her chin and spoke with an authority that I had not associated with her.

"The only thing we can say for sure is that the choice of topic might say something about a writer."

"So – now you're admitting that father might've invented the entire story."

"The entire story? It's possible," she said. "But the two extremes of absolute reality and absolute fantasy are rare. Stories usually reflect the range of possibilities that come in between."

"So are you saying...," I paused while the foghorn made a sound like a faraway lament. "Are you saying that there might be truth and fiction in the story but that we can't distinguish between the two?"

"You got it," Josie said. "But the parallels here are obvious, yeah? Fiction - the protagonist writes a verse from the *Rubaiyat* on the back of a postcard and gives it to his lover. The postcard turns up years later with a solicitor's letter. Fact - dad and N exchanged edelweiss and quotations from the *Rubaiyat* in August 1939. Seventy years later, one of these quotations turns up together with a dedication on the back of an old postcard of the *Kreuzberg*, yeah? The only difference between fact and fiction is, like, our postcard comes with edelweiss and a wreath from New York."

"OK, I wouldn't call this fact. I'd call it..."

"Just a minute," Josie said, holding out both arms. "Fact - the other quotation turns up in father's office a few days after the funeral. The quotation and the dedication, 'To CS with love from N. August 1939,' are written on a greeting card found in the casket I have with me today."

"I'd call it circumstantial evidence," I said.

Silence followed. Josie put her hands on her hips and Liz stepped between us.

"Siblings," she said. "No need to argue about this. There must be someone we can ask."

"We have a duty to take this story to dad's old agent," I said. "If he's still alive he might be able to tell us about edelweiss, the *Rubaiyat* and an enigmatic figure known as N."

Ben reappeared in the doorway. He was sobbing.

"He killed his daddy. He killed his daddy."

"Who killed his daddy, dear?"

"He killed his daddy."

"Maybe he didn't know who his daddy was, dear."

"Ask God to bring his daddy back; please, mummy."

"Nobody can do that, dear."

A ray of sunlight filtered through the lounge window and made pools of light on the carpet. Josie seemed shaken.

"I'd better go while the fog has cleared," she said.

We agreed that Josie would use her contacts to gain us an interview with father's former literary agent. A few minutes later, she was at the door.

"I'll be in contact when I've heard from him, Nicholas."

"I look forward to it," I said.

She smiled, and I felt the pressure of her hand on my forearm.

"Dad did pay maintenance, yeah?"

"Why is it important?" I asked.

"It's cool, really."

She removed her hand and set off towards the garden gate.

"By the way," I shouted after her, "feel free to call me Nick."

# 7

Outside the hut, the mountains appear and disappear with the rise and fall of the fog. Inside the hut, Josie is talking in her sleep again.

"Just read it," she says, "read it."

She is probably reliving in her dreams that afternoon in Southsea when we disagreed over fact and fiction in the last short story. Since we saw the items in the hotel cabinet 2 days ago, I have been forced to admit that elements of father's life are probably reflected in this piece. It is clear to us both that the casket Josie brought to Southsea once contained edelweiss. We also know that N died in 1991 and that father inherited money on N's death.

I still have doubts concerning the agent's claim that what happened in Germany in 1939 influenced everything father wrote. This claim may be nothing more than opinion. Nevertheless, I have tried to read *The White Mountain* with his comments in mind, and it is true that since our arrival in *Oberwald* 3 days ago, evidence of his claims has been easier to find.

It is now light enough for me to read *The White*

*Mountain* again. I open the book at the beginning and hold it close to the window. As a child, I read the prologue innumerable times and I always imagined the man climbing the mountain was my father and the woman was his lover. Both were still hiding out in the mountains and carrying on their struggle against evil. Since last night, the prologue has taken on a far more sinister meaning, and my childhood fantasies have been blown away.

> Darting upwards through the forest, she flitted from tree to tree and from sunlight to shadow. Her footfalls, cushioned on layers of leaves and pine needles, barely sounded in the rustling stillness. Abruptly, she halted and, like a deer that has caught scent of the hunter, she cocked her head and span round. Her companion was struggling. Fifty metres behind, he was gasping for breath on the steep mountain path. He looked up and sought her eyes with his. There was a pleading expression on his face that seemed to ask: Can't you see I'm doing my best? But a shadow of pain or sorrow darkened his features, and he turned his head away when it caught the full force of her withering stare. She placed her hands on her hips and urged the man on with a mouthed but silent cry.
>
> When he raised his head to wipe his forehead, the flickering shadow of a bird hovering overhead stopped him in his tracks. The bird was large, dark and menacing. Swooping up, down, and around the crags, it was alert to danger, protecting its young. Sometimes it paused in mid-

flight; hanging hunched and tense, before it dived again towards the rock face. The woman leaned forward and beat the palms of her hands upon her thighs. Panting, the man nodded and trudged on.

The sun had been high in the sky when they had set off from the valley. By the time they reached the nick in the ridge, daylight was fading fast. The sun was about to set, and an icy mantel of blue was spreading over the snow-covered mountains to the west. Far beneath them, and shrouded under a soft mist, was the forest they had passed through. Now turning early-spring green, it reached out like tentacles and gripped the rocky buttresses that grew majestically from the valley floor and rose beside them. Winding down the mountainside and trailing away into the trees was the path they had taken. Beside it, the dying light glinting off its waters, the stream rushed and tumbled down the Valley of Prisoners and plunged silently into the forest.

The woman stiffened and, urgently gripping her companion by the shoulder, she peered downwards. Leaning into the void, she held her breath and scanned the valley below. There was a flash of colour from amongst the trees. A second later it was there again. It was a flash of blue, a windcheater perhaps, and it was getting nearer. With an explosive string of curses, the woman straightened up. She swayed for a moment when a sudden gust of wind caught her off balance. She leaned forward as if the wind were a force against her will and then strode towards a boulder at the mountain edge.

Concern briefly registered in the man's eyes as he watched her drop to her knees. He took a sharp intake of breath when, with a suggestion of desperation, she clawed and scratched at the earth. He was about to move forward and help her when she raised something from the ground. The object was wrapped tightly in strips of white sheeting and looked like a relic from a mummy's tomb. She uncoiled the strips and raised the relic over her head. At that moment the object was a block of wood, pieces of metal and nothing more. It was an old bolt-action rifle she held, and the touch of it seemed to steady her. Turning, she thrust the rifle into the man's outstretched hands.

In one expert movement, he lifted the gun and drew the butt into his groin. Removing the clip with his free hand, he rolled his thumb over the top cartridge and pressed down on it to test the clip's spring. Smiling, he shoved the clip back into the magazine. He turned his head towards hers and raised his eyebrows. The woman opened her lips as if to speak, but before she uttered a sound, he lifted a finger to his lips and silenced her.

He turned towards the disembodied shouts and laughter that drifted across the upland. The man they had come to find was in the refuge that nestled in the shadow of a great tooth-shaped peak. Adjacent and glowing blood-red as it caught the last rays of sunlight, another great tooth rose like an obelisk.

I raise my head and look through the window and into the silence of approaching dawn. I feel excitement, a sense of anticipation before the sun rises. It is there now. I can see its light on the distant mountains, and the summit of the *Widderstein* is visible as a glowing candle above us. Excitement turns to fear when I settle my eyes on the book again. I want to read the rest of the prologue with the eyes of a child but I know what is coming. Someone needs to change the ending and rewrite history. But the agent said the book was a purging experience. Perhaps, everything we need to know is in *The White Mountain* after all, and there is nothing I can do to change it.

> The woman shivered in the wind and the gathering darkness. Clouds, which that morning had been tightly packed down on the horizon, were now billowing upwards and threatening to come down on them. Glancing down the valley, the woman saw the figure in blue emerging from the trees. Fifteen minutes more and the walker would be in close proximity.
>
> Seeing alarm in her eyes, the man brushed past. Dropping to his knees, he put out his hand and lowered himself so that he was flat upon the earth. He drew the rifle butt into his shoulder and pulled at the bolt. There was a metallic click as the cartridge was forced up by the clip's spring. He pushed the bolt forward with the palm of his hand, and the cartridge settled into its chamber. Then, as he curled his finger round the trigger, a ray of light from the

setting sun struck the barrel of the rifle. The woman let out a muted curse of irritation and raised her arm to shield her eyes from the blinding light.

The wind had dropped and droned in the crags. It was in this moment of stillness, a moment when the air of invisible things touched and shaped the ancient rock, that they heard a distant cry. It came across the emptiness from beyond the vanishing point of observation and prompted the man to look upwards with a bewildered expression in his eyes. The woman turned an ear into the whispering wind but before she could place the sound in space or time, the cry was taken up by the wind and carried away into the approaching dusk.

Suddenly agitated, the woman lifted her arm in the direction of the hut. She turned her eyes to his. Opening her mouth, she clipped the back of her teeth with her tongue and her lips came forward and closed around one long sound: "Now."

She looked towards the refuge. She barely had time to register that the dying rays of sunlight were glowing red in the thickening haze. Birds had taken to flight in a frenzy of squawking and beating of wings. It was their last desperate warning of a danger that threatened. The danger was now a sound that boomed and bounced off the mountain peaks. But the warning came too late for the person who lay face down on the refuge terrace. The hand was outstretched, and his blood dripped and drenched the earth under him. The block of wood and pieces of metal had become an assassin's weapon and now it would have to be buried.

Billowing clouds rolled over the plateau. The crags seemed to steam for a moment and then, the couple were plunged into mist. She pulled at the man's elbow. He rose and looked expectantly into her eyes. She beckoned, and without hesitation, he followed. She led the way to a narrow path that cut into the rock face, and in a second, they had vanished in the mist.

I close the book and let my fingertips run over its cover. The other two are still sleeping, but I am still anxious about the man and I need to be vigilant. I incline my head as if to hear some advice. There is silence from outside the hut and there is silence from within. It occurs to me that I would not have the book at all had Stefan not found it two days ago. We were on our way down from *Kreuzberg* when I heard a man's voice from behind.

\*

"Is this yours?"

We had barely reached the edge of town. The dirt track was already giving way to asphalt, and Josie was standing under a "Moka" sign that swung above the entrance to a bar not more than five metres away. She still had her back to me. In the distance, the church and the memorial to the mountain troops marked the entrance to *Oberwald*'s main square, but there was not a soul in sight.

"Hello? Is this yours?"

I span round. The man was standing in my shadow

and holding out a book.

"You must've dropped it on your way down," he said as I took *The White Mountain* from his hand. "Probably fell out of your side pocket."

He was around forty, looked fit and strong and was dressed in the fashionable gear of the 2-weeks-a-year mountaineer. I had not seen any local men with branded check shirts and matching socks. His eyes darted about below a black beret perched jauntily on his head. Beneath the beret, greying hair fell in curls over his ears. His face was open and friendly, and he spoke English with little accent.

"You passed me," he said. "I was sitting by the side of the track. Have you visited the memorial?"

I turned to look at the monument. It was standing proudly among the trees. There was a motionless figure beside it. No doubt it was a tourist, I thought, come to pay his or her respects.

"Yes, I think they come to remember. Peculiar, isn't it? As if we'd ever forget. We never escape from our forebears, whoever they are and whatever they've done."

While my thoughts danced briefly on the burden of guilt he was referring to, I sensed rather than saw the cloud shadow pushing in around us.

"So, what brings you here?" I said.

"I'm a journalist – from Munich. I cover all newsworthy stories in the Bavarian mountains. This means..."

A sudden movement from behind me interrupted him. He fidgeted, and his darting eyes slipped away from mine and took on a mischievous look.

"This means I come here about once a month. Name's Stefan," he said.

The smile which accompanied this introduction beamed past me and landed on a presence at my shoulder. Josie had crept up and was standing next to me.

"You know," he said, directing his words past my right ear, "there was a time when people came in great numbers to visit this monument. Few come now."

Josie emerged from my peripheral vision and stepped past me. Her hand alighted briefly on Stefan's arm.

"Name's Josie, yeah?"

Shuffling uncomfortably, I tried to ignore the air of complicity that surrounded them and was about to butt in and introduce myself when Stefan indicated the cross with a movement of his hand.

"In fact, he said, "so few come that the grave garden on the *Kreuzberg* isn't kept the way it was. Maybe when the last of us goes, the garden will merge into the hill, and the cross and the memories that are buried there will return to nothingness. Ashes to ashes, dust to dust."

Somewhere in the town a door slammed shut with a noise like a pistol shot. A pile of grit and dust blew up the street, and the "Moka" sign squeaked and swung in the blast of air. I felt my jacket tighten over my chest, and the branches of the trees that lined the road lifted like lids. The world was plunged back into a wintry dusk.

"When I see these distant figures on the hill," Stefan said, "a question always enters my head."

He bit his lower lip and hesitated into our silence.

"Do you know what that question is?" Stefan asked.

His eyes wandered to me, but I shook my head. I guessed that Stefan's "you" was singular and directed at Josie but she had removed her rucksack and was busy ignoring him by rearranging its contents.

"The question is this," Stefan said at last. "Why do they come? What do people hope to gain from a visit to a war memorial? What do you think?"

I was distracted by a number of old men, who had emerged from the bar. They were chatting and orchestrating their conversation with expansive gestures while a couple of dogs scurried amongst them.

"They come to pay their respects, yeah?"

Stefan folded his arms, apparently lost in contemplation of the sunlight and cloud shadow battling for possession of the ground around him.

"And what exactly do you mean by the word 'respect'?" he said. "Is it an appreciation of man's inhumanity to man or is it an appreciation of his instinct for survival? Or is it more than this?"

Josie was looking at Stefan in a way that evidently disconcerted him. He placed one hand on his beret and pulled it down further on his head. His curly hair was blowing tight against his temples.

"These four dead people," he continued, glancing at Josie, "these victims of war and tyranny. What do they represent? Are they simply a reminder of what man did to man? Do we come in the hope that should the same situation arise again, we'd behave differently?"

There was a rush of air followed by a deep vibration which sounded like distant thunder. I saw Josie part her legs to steady herself and her cagoule billowed outwards as it caught the buffeting wind. She then leaned over and busied herself with the rucksack again.

"You know," the journalist said, "the military has always claimed that they had nothing to do with those four deaths. They claim that on the night they died, there were no German soldiers stalking the streets of *Oberwald.*"

He stopped speaking for some moments and watched Josie play with the straps of her rucksack. He seemed to be deliberating with himself whether or not to continue.

"No," he said at length. "It's impossible to prove but I wonder if the only thing that stalked the streets that night was fear."

Stefan stepped backwards and beamed at both of us.

An expression in his eyes suggested he was expecting us to applaud his eloquence but a mild nervousness revealed itself in his clasped hands. He was rubbing them together and apparently protecting them from the worsening weather. The trees lining the road were hurling themselves from side to side as if they were intent on throwing off the grip of a predatory animal. Into these howls of anger, the journalist shouted:

"So, you've come to protest?"

I noticed that although his question was directed at me, his eyes were blank. I ducked as a small branch rushed with the wind and landed at my feet. Josie appeared to be considering his question but ended by shrugging her shoulders.

"A protest, yeah?"

Her words sounded challenging to me but Stefan's eyes flickered from side to side in confusion.

"There's to be a protest in the town," he said, giving up the pretence of including me in the conversation.

"How cool is that? About what?"

"So, you don't know?"

"You got it."

Stefan seemed pleased with this reply. He nodded towards the group of old men. They had drawn together and their conversation hung in the balance while the wind blew between them.

"Everyone in town's talking about it," he said. "The specific focus of the protest is the reunion."

There was a long pause, and I wondered whether he was looking for another round of applause. He glanced at me and scanned Josie's face for signs of understanding. Finding only a faint smile from me and a shake of the head from Josie, he said:

"Since 1952, *Oberwald* has hosted the reunion of the veterans of the *Gebirgsjager*, the elite mountain troops." His voice grew louder in an attempt to counter the sound of the rushing wind. "Every year, veterans and their families gather in the town where many of the regiments were raised. The protesters will draw attention to crimes committed during the war. These crimes include the killing of the civilians on the hill here."

For a moment there was only the sound of the wind rushing between us. A dog barked, the old men shifted uncomfortably, broke up and went their separate ways.

"The former West German authorities proved reluctant to punish those responsible for the crimes. It is significant that many of those who served in the division until 1945 went on to hold senior posts in government and in the newly formed *Bundeswehr*. And you know..."

Stefan was cut short by a ferocious gust of wind. He put his hand on his beret but the collars of his fashionable shirt flapped wildly. He made an expansive gesture with his arms.

"It's hardly surprising," he said, "that the official '64 investigations into the murders were abandoned. 'Lack of evidence,' they said."

Stefan looked at his feet and shook his head in a way that suggested he would shake away his own disbelief.

"So, what's new?" Josie said, suddenly animated. "Some people won't thank you for digging around in their past."

There was another distant rolling of thunder and its echo thumped around the mountain peaks. Stefan looked up and focused on Josie.

"It's complicated," he said to her. "Even if the soldiers deny responsibility for the four murders, there's another side to the protests. That side is..."

A shriek of wind silenced him, and I staggered forwards while my trousers flapped at my ankles. Into the unnatural stillness that followed, Stefan said:

"That side is cover up. *Oberwald*'s officials are inhibited about their Nazi past. They are worried about any revelations that could harm the town's image. It's understandable. The Alpine World Ski Championships will be held here next year. More importantly, a bid has been submitted to co-host the 2018 Winter Olympics. A successful bid would bring untold benefits to *Oberwald* and the local economy. New hotels, new conference centres, better rail connections to Munich..."

"And the past is kind of uncool, so it can be ignored, right?"

Stefan laid his finger across his mouth and allowed himself to gaze at her as if in reflection.

"Not quite right," he said. "Some aspects of the past are played up and others are played down."

"Which means?"

"The towns here are keen to play up the sporting aspects of the 1936 Winter Olympics, which were held down here. They are less interested in re-examining the political aspects of those games and their aftermath. Amongst those political aspects, the murder of the four people on the hill stands out."

I was about to jump into the conversation when I felt a splash on my forehead. I looked up at the sky. Clouds, swollen with rain water, sped above the town. Raindrops were hitting the dust and lay like ink spots. In a matter of seconds, the ground seemed diseased and pockmarked.

"What brings you here?" Stefan asked.

I opened and then closed my mouth. Neither Stefan nor Josie seemed interested in me. Her eyes were locked on to his and I was an intruder on a private conversation.

"We are here to scatter our father's ashes, yeah?"

Stefan allowed his gaze to wander over to me and then back to Josie.

"Why here?"

"It was part of his last will that his ashes be scattered on the *Widderstein* on 23 August."

"Tomorrow?" Stefan said. "It's a significant date."

Josie squinted at him.

"What do you mean by 'significant'?"

"The deaths of the people on the hill occurred on 16 August," Stefan said, the words running ahead of the wind. "And exactly one week later, on 23 August, there was another killing."

I felt the wind tugging at my legs, and the question on my lips was temporarily silenced by a necessity to keep my balance.

"Back to the hotel?" Stefan said.

The rain was now falling persistently and, without further words, we moved off down the street and into the main square. Between the church and the fountain, the rain came down in torrents and we made a dash for shelter. Ducking our heads and hunching our shoulders we arrived in the entrance hall of our hotel. We had barely caught our breath when the receptionist appeared. She apologised and informed us that the manager was unable to see us at 4.00 but that he would be happy to see us at 6.30 that evening if it was convenient.

Stefan was whispering in Josie's ear. I thought I heard him say:

"Meet me in the bar?"

"Cool. I'm up for it."

He brushed past me and, almost as an afterthought, he said:

"Seven-thirty, OK? I'll tell you what I know."

# 8

Josie appears calmer now and is sleeping noiselessly, but I cannot say what is happening in her dreams. I do know she is struggling with her dad's past. She was shaken by the details of his relationship with N and she is still finding her balance. But Josie is admirably resilient and already talking about how fulfilling a long-term relationship might be.

As for me, I just keep on asking questions. What do we really know about what happened in 1939? How accurate is Stefan's story of cover up? He says he is a journalist, and cover up is a popular theme among reporters and writers, a sure-fire hit that appeals to a reader's love of scandal and of outrage. And yet, cover up is a theme that permeates *The White Mountain*, and the parallels between Stefan's claims of wrongdoing and the plot of the novel are getting too similar for even an old stick like me to ignore.

I fumble for *The White Mountain* again and skim through it. In the book, there are frequent passages detailing attempts by the villagers to conceal their past crimes. Sergio gets his first insight into these guilty secrets when he visits the village priest in order to discuss complaints made against Caterina Bertone and her cats.


"These six dead partisans of *Quero Vas*," the priest continued, now looking up. "What do they represent to you?"

Sergio stepped hesitantly towards the centre of the room. His head was beginning to clear.

"You," the priest said, "you, of course, are too young to remember. You cannot be expected to recall the smell of fear that ran through the streets then. Perhaps it was nothing but fear that prompted men to kill and to be heroes."

"You were here in 1943?"

"Sometimes," the priest said, "I feel I've been here forever. I told you, Capitano, I have long since reached an age when the past is all I have."

Sergio saw the old man smile.

"And, Capitano," the priest said, suddenly serious, "you have to live with it. Whatever has happened, you have to live with it. There is nothing else."

Don Giuseppe appeared to scan the table in front of him. Then, he sat forward and placed his hands together on the top of his desk.

"But, Capitano," he said, "you are not here to listen to the reflections of a tired old man. That is not why you've come. Am I right?"

Sergio moved towards the shutters. He raised his arm and let his hand rest on a slat.

Pretending to look at the monument, he glanced at his watch. He would stay for 15 minutes, he told himself. Then he would collect an overnight bag and drive to Verona. He had not come to hear stories about the war. He was not part of this village where history brooded and where there was a pervasive sense of death. Spinning round, he sought out the priest's eyes.

"It's Caterina Bertone I want to talk about."

The priest made an almost imperceptible movement of his head. Sergio supposed it was a nod.

"And what, Capitano," the priest said, adopting an official tone, "what can I tell you?"

Stifling a feeling of irritation, Sergio took a deep breath.

"A complaint has been made against her," he said. "I need an independent view."

The priest sat still, his hands resting palms down on the table. For some seconds the silence between the two men was broken only by the clicking of cicadas basking in the sunlight outside. The priest lowered his head.

"Old stories," he said under his breath, "come to haunt us."

Sergio frowned.

"I need an independent view," he said, "because the other villagers are involved."

"Involved? And what exactly, may I ask, are they involved in?"

"That is why I have come," Sergio said.

"They are involved in the ignoring. They are involved in the not-caring. I thought maybe you could help me understand why."

The priest made a light movement of his shoulders and an almost inaudible sigh.

"Why did you think that? If there are any dark secrets here, do you believe I would tell you about them? I am the priest here. I hear the confessional."

Sergio blinked in astonishment at the priest's tone of quiet conviction. Nevertheless, he decided to press on.

"Caterina Bertone has no family?"

The priest spread his hands and shook his head.

"She's a recluse. Apart from her cats, she lives alone."

"Then she has no friends at all?"

"Only old Giovanni, but even he leaves her alone now."

"Why does she shy away from the other villagers?"

Don Giuseppe lowered his eyelids.

"She doesn't."

He leaned back in his chair. Raising his arms, he cupped the back of his head in his hands. He reflected for a while before continuing.

"It is she," he said, "who is shunned by the village."

"Why?"

Don Giuseppe leaned so far back that his face was lost in the shadows. When he spoke again, the disembodied voice was a whisper, and the priest isolated and extended each syllable.

"It was the war, Capitano, the war. She knew."

"Knew? What did she know?"

"She thought she knew the truth, Capitano." He leaned abruptly forward, and his face shot out of the darkness. "She thought she knew the truth about the partisans there on the hill. Yes, our partisans, Capitano, the heroic partisans of *Quero Vas*. Did you know that one of them was her brother?"

Don Giuseppe locked his hands together as if recharging his will.

"But you know how it is with these people here. I know everything. They confessed. I can tell you nothing more. You would not ask me to break faith."

The appeal to religious tradition, to authority beyond the reach of the law, irritated the policeman. He stepped aggressively towards the desk.

"Monsignor, I have a duty of care to all those who live in this village. A complaint has been made." Sergio felt more comfortable now that he was on familiar ground. He had a duty to perform. "I must do something."

Don Giuseppe seemed unmoved by Sergio's outburst. He smiled.

"Do?" he said. "Isn't it more important to think?"

"Maybe," said Sergio, managing a smile of his own, "but I am not paid to think. I am paid to act."

Sergio started slightly and, for a moment, neither man moved. Then, Sergio added:

"And I need to act as efficiently and as effectively as possible."

"Ah," the priest began with a nod of the head. "Efficient and effective. Yes, we know about these new Gods. I have read about them. But what about the human cost? What about the pain and the suffering? Isn't the price too high? And is it worth it? Eh? Can you tell me? Have you thought about it?"

The priest stared into Sergio's eyes.

"I told you, Capitano," he said slowly, "the past is all I have. There is nothing we can do to change it now. Shouldn't we leave the past alone?"

Don Giuseppe rose and moved towards the shutters, his cassock stroking the triangular tiles.

"Old stories come to haunt us," he muttered to himself.

He seemed to hesitate as if making a calculation. With a deliberate movement, Sergio looked at his watch and then at the priest. Don Giuseppe lifted his chin and spread his hands in resignation.

"I will tell you this and this only, Capitano. And when I have told you, I will tell you no more. You are free to do what you like with the information, but it will make no difference now. The past has happened and history is written."

His face broke into another smile.

"But as you know, Capitano," he said, "history is always written with the present in mind."

Sergio glanced again at his watch. The priest turned his gaze to the floor.

"The night the partisans died," he said, "there were no Germans near this village."

He stopped speaking for some moments. Sergio felt that Don Giuseppe was conversing with some inner voice.

"No," the priest said at length. "They were not here physically, I mean. But the fear, the fear of what they would do to us if they knew we helped a band of partisans..."

Sergio waited with open mouth. For several seconds he heard nothing except the heat crackling on the outside walls of the house. He was wondering whether Don Giuseppe had finished with his story when the priest raised his eyebrows and looked him straight in the eye.

"The fear was with us then," he said, "and it has never left us."

Putting out his arm, Don Giuseppe rested his hand on the shutters. He peered through the slats at the cross on the hill.

"Our memorial is important to us. It tells us we are human. It reminds us."

"And Caterina Bertone," Sergio said, "what does she have to do with all this?"

Don Giuseppe pondered for a moment before replying.

"I have told you, Capitano, nothing more. Caterina Bertone is a recluse. She prefers the company of cats. What more can anyone tell you? The past is all I have. We should leave it alone."

There was an expression in the priest's eyes that suggested he had nothing more to say.

I snap the book shut. The similarities between Stefan's story and the plot of the novel are striking, but they do not constitute hard evidence. In the same way, although my half-siblings share their names with the victims memorialised on the *Kreuzberg*, it is not incontrovertible proof that father named his children in their honour.

Most of the evidence concerning Josie's "dark and long silence" is circumstantial. The agent's claim that writing *The White Mountain* was a purging experience for its author might be true, but there is nothing to prove it, and I currently have more urgent and concrete things to think about.

I am concerned about the other man in this hut. What he knows and what he decides to do about it are too unpredictable to even contemplate. I am concerned about Josie and whether she will be well enough to go down the mountain today. I am concerned about the reasons why Josie and I once allowed ourselves to be controlled by our father's absence. Allowing him to pull the strings, we drifted into situations neither of us wanted to be in.

If I adopted Josie's rosy view of the world, I would say that father's death was a catalyst, and our decision to talk to father's former agent earlier this summer was, perhaps, the first step towards taking control of our own lives. It was also this visit that sent us helter-skelter down the path that led to this hut with no people, this hut with no name.

Before we met that July morning, I did my homework. Josie is, as Liz discovered, the editor of the Exeter-based magazine: *The Good Housekeeper*. When she accepted this position, drastic action was needed to turn a dinosaur-like publication into something which reflected the contemporary world.

Josie set about sharpening the appeal of the magazine

by focusing on the modern woman and her daily concerns. The publication now offers diet plans, hair styling tips, travel ideas and support for single mums and women juggling a career with motherhood. By encouraging her readers to write in with questions, suggestions, poetry, stories, and household advice, Josie has succeeded in giving a new readership the feeling that they are participating in the creation of the magazine.

When I met Josie in the middle of July, she was planning the launch of the website: *Mumscompany.co.uk*, and she had an afternoon appointment with her financial backers in Tottenham Court Road. First, we both had an appointment with father's literary agent.

*

"What are we expecting from the agent?"

I asked this of Josie while we ambled through Russell Square, taking in the summer haze that hung in the trees and avoiding the power walkers who bore down on us along the perimeter path. Six weeks had passed since her visit to Southsea and, although we had been in regular email contact, there had been no more surprises from father's office. It turned out that Josie had been "under pressure" at work and Miriam had been on a 2-week training exercise in Germany with her unit of the Territorial Army. There was still "...like, a mountain of documents to sieve through," Josie told me. When we arrived beside the Cafe in the Square, she said:

"I'm expecting him to shed some light, Nick."

The smile that accompanied these words began as a tug at the corners of her mouth and it pressed her cheeks up to reveal her teeth. By the time the smile crinkled her eyes, I realised she was reacting to the pleasure I felt on hearing my nickname and which probably showed on my face.

"Light on the dark silence?" I suggested.

A flicker in Josie's eye acknowledged my reference to her dark and long silence, and we set off across the terrace towards an empty table. The nodding heads of other customers followed Josie's poise and grace, but her face was turned towards me, and I got a sense of how it must be for a supporting actor bathing in the charisma of his leading lady.

"I'd better bring you up to speed, yeah?"

I caught a waiter's eye and slid sideways onto the seat opposite Josie. She was sitting with a view of the square, and her eyes were criss-crossing its open areas in the manner of searching lights. Leaning forward, I placed my elbows on the table top and cupped my chin in my hands. Although she looked as if she had stepped out of one of her magazine pictures, she allowed her own person to shine through the conservative grey of her business suit. It was in the blush of the cheeks, the colour on her fingernails, and the matching splash of green in her ball of hair.

She told me that the agent, with whom she had made our appointment, was the son of the man who had represented our father.

"He didn't, like, make a big thing about it."

"About the story, you mean?"

Josie pursed her lips and made a non-committal movement of her head.

"He just commented that today's reader has, like, never heard of a has-been like Charles Saddler."

She gazed into my eyes until I lifted my chin and allowed my forearms to topple towards the salt and pepper. Rolling my head away from Josie's searching eyes, I scanned the tables around us. I was struck by the sensation that I was performing on stage while the other customers on the cafe terrace listened to every word and were attentive to every slip and hesitation.

"Don't be too disappointed, Nick. The story was only going to be, like, an entrance ticket, yeah?"

I looked down at my hands and found them lightly clenched but unfurling on the table top. I managed to avoid further searching of Josie's eyes by turning my head towards the arrival of Luca, the Italian waiter. He was in his early thirties, powerful and broad in the shoulder, and he hovered over Josie with movements that suggested suppressed energy. Josie ordered *espressi* and a bottle of mineral water for us. Luca backed away muttering: "Si, signora." When he was out of ear-shot, Josie said:

"How cool is that?"

"What?"

"The waiter. I was like – wow, that could be Sergio from *The White Mountain*."

"Josie, please..."

"Perhaps this is where the guy ended up, yeah? Accused of a crime he never committed, he fled to England."

"Why don't you write a sequel?"

She reached over the table and put her hand over my wrist.

"Nick, get real; nobody's interested anymore. Charles Saddler's had his day."

Her hand did not move; it was my turn to say something and the audience was expectant.

"Was Sergio another product of father's imagination?"

"Perhaps, he was kind of based on a homesick waiter dad met in London, yeah?"

"That would fit with father's themes; the loneliness of existence right up to a penniless, arthritic and bitter end."

Josie slid her hand away and held it out, palm

upwards in the manner of a beggar.

"Unless he's kind of dramatically rescued at the last moment, yeah? A letter arrives from the US, and..."

The rattle and ring of china and spoon announced the return of Luca. With a tray balanced on an outstretched hand, he swayed around Josie. It seemed to me that he might be an out-of-work model or actor. Neither his face nor his movements contradicted this possibility, and he laid our table with the movements of a graceful dancer. He ignored me altogether and when he had finished, he backed away muttering, "*Prego, signora, prego signora.*"

"You said the last story was an entrance ticket?"

"To hear about the story's author. Are you up for it?"

I put both hands together and slid them between my thighs.

"Absolutely. So, what are our aims?"

Josie leaned forward and, resting her elbows on the table top, she placed the palms of her hands together and steepled her fingers.

"To gather information about what dad did in Germany in 1939?" Josie suggested. "Why was he there and who did he meet?"

"Are his novels autobiographical?" I countered.

A shadow spread over us. Luca had returned and was standing next to Josie. She glanced at him, shook her head and opened her praying hands.

"I'll write the questions down, yeah?"

Luca sidled away while Josie dug a pencil from her bag and slid a paper serviette across the table towards her. While I watched her bowed head following the movements of the scribbling lead, I asked myself whether our relationship would have developed this far had we not been siblings with a common goal.

"What about your brothers and sisters," I said. "Are they not interested in your dad's life?"

Josie looked up.

"Perhaps when their nests are empty and their careers are kind of over."

"I take that as a 'no' then."

"I hope they don't leave it too late, yeah? They'll find that our long and dark silence will've been sucked into a deep black hole. That's not cool."

I looked at her and wondered whether we knew each other well enough for my next question.

"What about you, Josie? Did you never consider marrying, then?"

An unnatural silence seemed to fall over the cafe terrace. It was the silence of the expectant audience sitting back and waiting to see what would happen next. While I fumbled in my pocket and dropped a handful of coins on the table, I sensed disapproval on the faces of the people around me. By the time I was on my feet, I was expecting them to start booing. I barely registered that our paper-serviette questionnaire was still lying on the table when I set off after the running woman and followed her across the square.

# 9

The book is open and roof-like over my thigh, and my hands are clasped together and rest on the book's spine but I am looking through the window and into the silence. Not so long ago, the distant mountains were ill-formed shapes that resembled clouds in the sky. Now, the haze is lifting, and clefts and valleys are revealing themselves. I want to reach out and touch them.

Reflecting on our visit to father's former agent, I see how he helped us recognise themes in *The White Mountain* that once passed us by. Concealment of past crimes is no longer new, but we had never considered father's fear of retribution. The irony is that I am sitting in this hut with similar concerns. Fear of retribution has been with me the whole night and is still there at dawn. Fear of retribution permeates *The White Mountain*.

I lift the novel from my thigh, turn it over and skim through its pages until I find the relevant chapter. Scanning its paragraphs, I pick out the key words "guilt," "lies," "deception" and "fear." Sergio has discovered that the partisans memorialised on *Monte Croce* were not killed by the Germans but by the townsfolk. Beatrice, with whom he has become romantically involved, tells him that he should reveal the truth to the world. But Sergio is aware of the consequences of any such revelation.

Sergio had gone no more than a few metres past the chapel when an overpowering tiredness slowed his pace to a trudge. The sight of the village lights, twinkling sparsely through the cypress trees, encouraged him to falter still further so that he resembled a man dragging his feet through the water. Considering what he had experienced that day, Sergio did not question his reluctance to hurry. The village offered him no refuge from the persistent feeling that he was carrying the virus of some deadly disease, and the villagers offered no protection from Spilimbergo and his threats.

Sergio scarcely noticed the farm houses that marked the furthest edge of *Quero Vas*. He was focused instead on an emotion which had already taken root inside him and which, to his surprise, had reached a new level of intensity. Disdain for the villagers had become a devouring contempt. "There is no reason why I should deal with this alone," he said to himself. "These people should answer for the crime of murder even if it happened a long time ago."

He would share his disease with them all, a small portion to each of them so that they would be reminded of their past crimes and share the burden of guilt. He walked on with a languid step until a grim thought stopped him dead in his tracks. "If they won't work with me, then I shall have to reveal the truth myself."

As soon as he had admitted the unthinkable, Sergio quickened his pace as if to run away from the idea. And yet, by the time he arrived in the square, he was amazed to discover that he felt comfortable with himself. He lifted his head and surveyed the village. Facing him, and glistening in the cold blue light of the moon, the church and the mountains both towered over *Quero Vas*. The houses were dark shapes that appeared to be crouching defensively, and Sergio was assailed by the absurd idea that something evil might jump out of the houses and attack him. He supposed it was a simple dread of the unknown, and he put out his hand and rested it on the familiar but cold, grey stone of the memorial.

"What is it that I am afraid of?" Sergio asked himself. "What is so difficult about revealing the truth?"

It occurred to him that the fear he felt was the same that he had experienced the previous evening. It was fear at the absence of a strong voice inside his head. He yearned for such a voice to guide him, to tell him how to act and what to believe in a world which offered so many choices. He was on the point of dashing to his car and driving away from *Quero Vas* when he hesitated, uncomfortably aware that the attention of person or persons unknown was centred on him. He allowed his eyes to flicker from side to side, breathed in the cool evening air, and told himself to throw these imaginary fears from his head. But there was nothing imaginary about the eyes that peered at him through the night. These eyes, frozen in time, gazed out at him from the photographs that decorated the memorial stone. "Lies and deception," they seemed to be saying. "Was it these for which we and the partisans died?"

The fixed expressions of the dead soldiers gripped him and prevented him from movement as though he too had become lifeless. With a strangled cry, Sergio snatched his hand away from the memorial. He had to admit that he envied those young and shining dead faces. There had been no choice for them, and they had become heroes.

"Then, perhaps I am a coward," Sergio thought, "and it is myself I am afraid of."

I look up. There are sounds of movement in the air outside the hut: the sigh of wind in the crags, the whistle of a bird calling to its mate and the tinkling of water from the melting snow. I am expecting my two companions to wake at any time. I hear them throwing off the deepest of sleeps. Two days ago, I was in my hotel room and listening to different sounds: the wind blowing through the square and muted words from somewhere in the town.

*

I had just turned fifty when I discovered the delights of the afternoon snooze. Mattresses were at their most inviting during the daylight hours, especially following a walk up a mountain like the *Kreuzberg*. Awaking after a nap, I was usually refreshed but I often felt traces of guilt, as if I had got away with doing something morally suspect.

On my second afternoon in *Oberwald*, I woke up cursing the luminous hands of my bedside clock. The hands glowed at me through the semi-darkness and accused me of oversleeping by 20 minutes. Reaching for the phone, I dialled Josie's room and arranged to meet her in the bar at 6.20. Then, I settled my head on the pillow and listened to the wind pulling at the shutters of the windows. I stayed in a remote state for some minutes but the memory of Stefan's words prompted me to swing my legs from the bed to the floor. "On 23 August, there was another killing."

I sat for a moment on the edge of the mattress and shook my head to clear it. I strode to the window, pulled it open and thrust my neck forward to peer through the shutter slats. Someone was standing outside the hotel. The slats cut the person into strips and, in the bottom strip, a pair of trousers was flapping in the wind. I watched the shoes swivel and the knees bend. A man's voice shouted:

"*Edelweiss  –  Totenweiss.  Gebirgsjaeger –  Totenjaeger,*" and the cry was taken up and echoed by a number of unseen people. "*Edelweiss* – deathweiss. Mountain troops – death troops." I drew back in alarm as though the words were directed at me. Leaning forward again, I saw that the legs were gone.

I pushed at the shutters. The rain had stopped, and *Oberwald* jumped out of the bright and watery light of late afternoon and confronted me with a babble of voices. The babble had no apparent origin and yet it spread outwards, over the rooftops and the narrow streets until it reached me. Leaning out of the window, I saw a veil of mist hanging over the left side of the square and, through the mist, I noted that a large number of people had herded together and were standing around in groups. The placards leaning against walls suggested that these were the protesters Stefan had mentioned. They looked passive enough, but the figures in black, dancing from one group to another with the nervous energy of blackbirds, suggested the expression "hard-core activists."

I was about to draw my head in when a flash of light in the distance caught my attention. Rings of mist were rising over the slopes of the *Kreuzberg*. Suspended between two such circles, the summit cross glinted like an evening star, but a cloud passed over the sun, the town was plunged into shadow, and the cross melted away into the hilltop. Simultaneously, the babble of voices from the square changed its tone. It became impatient and angry. Rising from it came a harsh and amplified voice: *"Edelweiss – Totenweiss. Gebirgsjaeger – Totenjaeger.*

I span round, strode across the room and pushed through the door into the corridor. I was down the stairs in a flash and found Josie waiting in the vestibule. She looked tense and uncomfortable, an impression in keeping with the air of expectancy that pervaded the entire ground floor. Knots of guests had gathered in and around the bar. Their talk and laughter were unnaturally loud, and eyes constantly flickered towards the hotel entrance. The fixtures and furniture from the entrance porch had been removed and the glass doors and nearby windows were taped up.

The hotel manager popped up from behind the reception desk when Josie and I approached. Dark-suited, sharp and efficient, he added two fire extinguishers to a grouping that stood sentinel at one end of the counter. He looked into Josie's eyes, held their questioning gaze for a moment, and said:

"No, we're not expecting trouble. It's just a precautionary measure to ensure the safety of our guests."

He apologised for his non-appearance earlier that afternoon, but the smile which followed was synthetic, and the eyes, which refused to meet ours, were cold.

"So," he said, "what can I do for you, ladies and gentlemen?"

Josie stared optimistically into his face while his smile rippled and then vanished. I broke in with a prompt.

"We spoke yesterday," I said. "About our father."

The manager interrupted me with a raised finger.

"Charles Saddler?"

"That's right," Josie said. "He stayed here in ...."

The manager nodded in time to Josie's rhythm and picked up her words so that when she reached the date, they were already a duet.

"In 1939," they said.

The manager was still nodding when he added:

"We've good news and bad news. The bad news is that..."

At that moment the door to the function room opened. The beat of jazz music emerged along with a lively chatter and a clinking of glasses. Rows of military medals glinted in the light from the chandeliers. The door closed to an escalation of anxious comments from around the bar, but the hotel manager remained cool.

"The bad news," he said, "is that it's impossible to say who was here at that time. The records were destroyed in 1945."

He spread his hands on the desk and wagged his head as an indication that the events of that time were not in his control.

"The good news is that post-war records reveal that

Mr Saddler was a frequent guest at this hotel in the late 1940s and the 1950s."

The door to the function room opened again, and music swung out into the entrance hall and invited us all to dance to its rhythm.

I drew out my father's 1939 photos and laid them on the counter.

"This is the hotel, isn't it?"

The manager glanced at the photos, and then examined some of them with apparent interest. In particular, he hovered over the shot of father and his soldier companions on the hotel terrace. Then, he slid the photos back to me, the expression on his face suggesting he had been handling something unpleasant. He shook his head.

"There are only respectable guests in our hotel now."

"Really?" Josie said. "Let me tell you something."

She lifted her hand, jabbed at the photograph with a fingernail and then indicated the function room with a reproaching finger.

"The boys in this shot could be in that room now, yeah?"

Somehow, the manager stuck to his performance but his reception desk looked increasingly like a barricade.

"At the moment we are preparing ourselves for next year's championships. But most importantly, we are preparing ourselves should the 2018 Olympic bid be successful. We are doing well. In fact, the town has done well in coming to terms with its past."

Josie was not to be put off so easily.

"The reunion must be an embarrassment to you, yeah?"

"It has been held here since 1952. It is a tradition. But the hotel's policy is now under review. We have to think about the future. This year might well be the last reunion. People are getting old."

"Well, just kind of brush it all under the carpet, then."

Josie illustrated this statement with a sweeping movement of the arm that began over her head, swung in a wide arc and ended with the arm across the opposite shoulder. While she tilted her chin upwards and looked down her nose at the manager, the function room door closed again, and the music abruptly stopped while in full swing. The manager glanced at his watch.

"We must move on," he said. "That brings me to more good news. Follow me please."

He swept out from behind his barricade and ushered us into the hallway. We followed him down a couple of flights of stairs and we drew up in front of a wall cabinet next to the sauna area.

"These are oddities from the family collection," he said. "In 1991, my grandfather received this letter from an old client. His name was Charles Saddler - your father, I believe."

We stared through the glass. At first, all I saw was the reflection of the manager standing at my elbow. Then, against his reflection, I saw the edelweiss flower. It could so easily have been the same small plant that fluttered from an envelope at father's funeral reception. But I connected these oblong leaves in the cabinet with the jewellery box Josie had found in father's office. The box had contained a card with a quotation from Omar Khayyam on one side and the words, "To CS with love from N. August 1939," on the other. I had always suspected that the jewellery box once contained an edelweiss flower and here it was in this cabinet and lying across the bottom corner of a letter.

> August 1991
> Dear Max
> This is the edelweiss I have told you about. It was given to me by an *Oberwalder*

friend with whom I climbed the *Widderstein* in August 1939. Nicholas recently died, and I feel that the edelweiss should be back in the mountains where it belongs.

Yours sincerely
Charles Saddler

With a noisy intake of breath, Josie backed away from the cabinet and scanned the floor at her feet as though looking for something she had dropped. I concentrated instead on the style of writing exhibited in the letter. Right-slanted and curving upwards at the end of each line, there was no doubt it was father's writing and it did not help me suppress a succession of images of him in the arms of another man. I decided to budge these images with the sound of my voice.

"Max was your grandfather?"

"That's right," he said. "He died in 2000."

A rustle at my elbow forced me to turn. Josie was holding out her arms in the manner of a Buddha and shaking her head in disbelief.

"Is that it?"

"I'm sorry you're disappointed, my lady."

"So, this is the famous N, yeah?"

Her tone suggested disappointment but I saw pain on the furrows that wriggled across her brow. Tears welled up in her eyes, and the manager turned to go.

"I'm sorry I can't be of further assistance."

He strutted off towards the staircase, and Josie strutted after him. When we arrived on the ground floor, the sight of a running woman click-clicking through the bar area was too much for guests expecting the hotel to be overrun by anarchists at any moment. Nervous chatter turned to alarm, and several women jumped to their feet and covered their mouths as if ready to scream. I hovered while Josie clattered into the empty porch and disappeared into the street.

"It all right," I said to the other guests. "She's upset. It's OK."

I rushed through the hotel entrance and turned left. The church clock was striking 7.00 when I arrived in the main square. The clouds were dispersing, and Josie had come to a halt about 20 metres in front of me with her head raised to the lightening sky. A breeze blew through the branches of the trees, the protesters were nowhere to be seen and an unnatural stillness hung over the town. I watched two walkers pass me by. They were laughing, and their cheeks were flushed and healthy. They marched past the fountain and made their way between the church and the memorial to the mountain troops and disappeared along the road that led to the *Kreuzberg*.

When I refocused on the square, Josie was nowhere to be seen. My gaze drifted from the fountain, to the memorial and then to the entrance to the church. The twitch of a curtain and the closing door suggested that someone had passed through, and I set off towards it.

At the push of my hand, enormous metal hinges creaked, and the door opened onto a dimness that glittered with gold and flickered with candles. A piece of curtain stroked my shoulder and fell back to the doorway. I saw Josie immediately. She was sitting in the front pews and facing a Christ figure hanging above the altar. Her legs were drawn beneath her and her shoulders were hunched. Clasping and unclasping her hands, she was looking to the floor as if ashamed to meet the eyes of the Christ figure towering over her. I took a few steps up the nave but a whisper reached out to me and stopped me in my tracks. At first, I thought the voice was simply one of many murmured prayers that collected here over the course of a day.

"Does it get kind of easier 6 months on?"

From the corner of my eyes, a shadow flitted; I heard a muffled footstep and the click of a closing door.

"Not really. Not for me. In fact, it..."

The voice was absorbed into other voices that hoped, dreamed and confessed and filled the space under the vaulted roof. I crept further up the nave until I was within touching distance of Josie. I saw her lips move but her voice was almost inaudible.

"After a couple of months, I thought the pain was easing," she said. "I stopped thinking of my father as a dead man in the morgue. I got more normal images when I thought about him: my father sitting on my bed telling me stories; my father at his desk; my father telling one of his jokes."

She raised her head and looked up at the Christ figure.

"But what really hurts," she whispered, "is that these memories were kind of fake. They were an idea of the person I wanted him to be and not the person he was."

She paused, but when I sat down beside her, she barely acknowledged my presence.

"But now I'm going through another phase of intensity. It started a few weeks ago and it's getting worse. Everything reminds me of him and all my thought processes lead me to him. When I'm sad about something, I remember dad because he was the person I wanted to go to for advice. He was never there. When I'm happy about something I remember dad because he was the person I wanted to share my happiness with. But he was never there."

She took a deep breath and with barely concealed spite, she said:

"So, now I'm kind of like, 'where were you, dad?'"

She let her question hang in the air as if unwilling to hear the answer spoken aloud. She recoiled as though shocked at her own thoughts and then said:

"Where were you? Trawling the toilets and picking up rent boys in Piccadilly Circus?"

"Stop it," I said. "We don't know whether he was gay or not. We don't know whether his relationship with Nicholas was a one-off. Maybe, he was bisexual. We just don't know."

"You don't need evidence. Just imagination, yeah?"

"Then don't let your imagination carry you away. We simply don't know anything."

I stamped my words with a finality that would discourage further useless speculation but Josie had gone off on a tangent.

"And, yes, he named us after those victims on the *Kreuzberg*. But what should I feel? Pride? Am I up for that? I mean, up for being a replacement for someone who was murdered over 70 years ago? He must have been ashamed of what I was, yeah? I can kind of write about mums, but I am not capable of being one."

"Bollocks," I said. "That is bollocks... bollocks..."

I said the word with such force that its echo, like a guilty confession, bounced around the vaulted roof and refused to go away. She looked sideways at me as though she had become aware of my presence for the first time.

"You know," she said, "when he was at home, I made myself pretty just to get his attention, just to please him. How ridiculous is that?"

I shook my head and caught her eye.

"What did your mum make of it all?" I asked.

"She knew, yeah? Before she died, she told us that he showed no sexual interest in her at all. Now it all kind of makes sense."

"When did she die?"

"1992."

"It's more likely that he was bi-sexual," I said.

"I'm cool about his sexuality. Are you?"

I looked into her eyes and wondered whether it was the right time to tell her that I had known for several weeks that N was a man.

"It's not a surprise," I said.

She looked at me closely.

"How long have you known?"

"It was in the 1948 letter," I said. "There is the tell-tale word 'him' and I knew then."

A number of emotions passed over Josie's face but she clearly decided to let the subject be. I knew as well as she did that withholding information from another person was tantamount to lying.

"Father left in 1960," I said. "I spent 10 years mourning his passing. Whether he was gay or not gay makes no difference to anything."

Josie looked down at her hands and said:

"Then I want to tell you something else."

"Go ahead," I said.

"When mother died, we found something that kind of saddened my father. She had a personal bank account containing about 25,000 pounds."

Josie placed the palms of her hands together and slid them between her knees.

"We estimate that this sum is equivalent to what should have been paid to you and your mother, yeah?"

Damp staleness seemed to radiate from the walls and touched my body. From the corner of my eye I saw Josie watching me as though she was searching for anger or hurt that might match her own.

"My mother says maintenance was never paid," I said with a force that surprised me. "Perhaps she wanted to believe this. It confirmed her belief that he was a bad man."

"No worries. You're not bitter?"

"It doesn't matter anymore," I said. "What about you? How do you feel?"

"I'm envious."

I blinked and looked at her profile. A tear was rolling down her cheek.

"Of what?"

"Sixty years of trust. Am I up for that sort of commitment?"

I looked up at the statue of Christ above the altar. He had not moved. I put my arms around Josie and tried to comfort her.

"It's not too late to change," I said.

While she cried into my shoulder, my own feelings told me that the maintenance issue mattered hugely. She must have felt it too and she lifted her hand and laid it on my head while I sobbed into her shoulder.

# 10

The air outside the hut seems fresh and clear. Below us, a bluish haze separates the mountain summits from their lower slopes, so that the peaks appear to be floating in the sky. I wonder whether I can really smell the melting snow. Perhaps, its presence is being suggested by the response of my old knees to the cold and damp.

Nearby grunts and whimpers suggest that Josie is being troubled by dreams again. I see them in her restless eyes and limbs. They suggest she is on the run from something dark and frightening. My guess is that this might turn out to be something she already glimpsed in the New York wreath and its attached quotations from her long and dark silence. She ran away from it last July when I questioned her about marriage. She ran away from it two days ago when she read the letter in the cabinet. I hope that, in this current dream, she will turn to face her menacing pursuer and ask it to reveal itself. I am sure it will say, "Commitment."

The power of fear has appeared frequently since father's funeral: fear of the dark, fear of the wicked acts we are capable of, and fear of vengeance. But until we visited father's former literary agent, Josie and I were unaware of my father's fear that the past might come back and bite him in the shape of reprisals. Nor had we guessed that it was fear of these reprisals that prompted father to "cover his tracks" and set *The White Mountain* in a fictional village in another country.

Rereading the book, I am struck by the frequency with which fear of exposing the truth appears. Sergio is uneasy at being in possession of information that suggests the villagers murdered the partisans, but when he announces his intention of revealing his findings to the world, the priest warns him that such an action might have dire consequences. My guess is that Sergio's conversation with the priest was one my father had with himself.

> The hand that touched Sergio's arm remained there a little longer before retracting into the sleeve of a black cassock. The priest's eyes, partly shaded by a black and wide-brimmed hat, were focused on some point in the distance. Following the direction of his gaze, Sergio saw the priest was looking at *Monte Croce*. The monument on the summit was glinting in the late morning sun.
>
> "As you know, Capitano," Don Giuseppe said, "the memorial was erected for the partisans, who were cut down by the Germans in 1943. This is the truth, Capitano. It has been permanently set down in ink for the sake of posterity."
>
> The inner quietness which had begun to descend on Sergio slipped away with the priest's insistent words, and the resentment

which followed produced a sulky silence. The priest said:

"So, you think you have discovered another truth. You think you know what really happened?"

Sergio said nothing. For a moment, there was a deathly hush between the two men, and Sergio had a morbid vision of those youngsters locked in a cellar and waiting for the grenades to explode.

"You are angry, Capitano," the priest said. "You are angry that such a thing can happen, am I right?"

There was a low mumbling from the bar. With his inner eye, Sergio saw the old villagers playing their games. It was obscene that their lives should continue as normal while his would be forever tainted. Eventually the priest said:

"Such things have happened before and they will happen again. You have to live with it."

Refusing to meet the priest's eyes, Sergio turned his face to the ground.

"You have missed the point," he said. "It needn't have happened like that."

"And I have told you," the priest said, "that it would be better to leave the past as it is."

"I have a duty," Sergio said, "to discover and tell the truth."

"So, you don't want to believe that the circumstances of those deaths are what you have been told?"

Swallowing down his growing anger and keeping his eyes firmly fixed on the ground,

Sergio said:

"Murder should be exposed and the murderers should be punished."

Don Giuseppe crossed his arms and placed both hands into the sleeves of his cassock.

"Do you believe in God, Capitano?"

Sergio blinked and looked up. In the powerful glare of the midday sun, he could hardly make out the priest's features. Only the cassock seemed real, and that was threadbare and frayed at the edges.

"I can neither prove nor disprove the existence of God," Sergio said.

The priest hesitated. The heat and humidity were stifling. Don Giuseppe took two steps into the shade of a tree and, tucking his cassock beneath him, he sat down on the bench.

"That is not what I asked," he said. "Do you or do you not believe in God?"

"Yes, I..."

"Then, you must believe in truth, beauty and good."

The policeman followed the priest into the shade of the tree. Even in the shadow, it was airless and scorching. Sergio took a deep breath.

"If I didn't believe in truth and good," he said, "I wouldn't be a policeman."

Don Giuseppe lifted a trembling arm and removed his hat.

"But truth and good are scarcely less ephemeral than the flowers, Capitano. What was true yesterday is not true today. Has it never occurred to you that good is nothing more than the conduct which fits the circumstances? Perhaps these villagers needed to survive. They are simple people but they are not stupid. Failure or success in their struggle for survival is the only moral standard in this place. During the war years, good to them was what survived. There is nothing more for them, Capitano."

Sergio shook his head.

"It is my duty to reveal the truth."

The priest was silent for a while. Then, he said:

"Perhaps the exploration of these people's thoughts and feelings is the next quest for you. Try and understand them."

"Them?"

"The villagers, Capitano. You talk as if there is nowhere to go but backwards. I am an old man, but for me too, a new adventure begins every day even though old habits and memories survive."

"So, are you saying I should let them get away with murder – murder of their own folk?"

"It was not murder to them," said the priest quickly, "they made their own rules for preservation."

"They are not above the law," Sergio said, "nor are they above conscience."

"You must recognise their rules, Capitano. Individuals who do not recognise them will be restrained."

"Like Caterina Bertone?"

The priest shook his head.

"If you interfere with their truth, do not complain if this society punishes you,

Capitano. You have been warned. The heroic partisans were cut down by the Germans in 1943. Caterina Bertone was a recluse who preferred the company of cats. This is the truth. Everyone says so. It is an accepted truth, self-evident and obvious."

I snap the book shut and still my renewed concern that I too might be about to suffer the punishment of revenge at the hands of this man sleeping near me. But my fear of vengeance is evaporating with the sunlight. Perhaps I am imagining it all. Perhaps it is the agent's fault for putting these ideas into my head. Neither Josie nor I knew anything of fear and retribution when we stood outside the publisher's offices that morning in mid-July.

*

The offices of Peter Germaine & Son, Literary Agents, were housed in a Georgian building on the museum side of Russell Square. The door was opened by a man dressed entirely in black. He was thin and severe, his face all downward tilts, his fine grey hair pulled into a tight pony tail. Ushering us in, he showed us into his office. The two chairs, lined up in front of his desk, invited us to use them, and Josie and I sat down when the agent did. He was brisk and business-like, but once he had settled in his chair, he became as still as a Buddha.

"Got the manuscript?"

He sounded like a criminal asking us if we had brought his money but the hair suggested to me that perhaps he was a corrupted hippy who had long since sold out to the capitalists and lost his dreams.

Josie leaned over the desk and put the foolscap paper into the agent's hand. Without a word, the man rose and disappeared through a door behind him. A muffled conversational exchange reached out to us. I tried to catch Josie's eye. I wanted to apologise for asking personal questions and upsetting her, but the muffled voices ceased, and the agent, now empty-handed, swept back into our room.

"My father will see you in a few minutes," he said, taking his seat again. "Please be aware that, other than a handful of academics, very few people will be interested in the piece. Charles Saddler's crime stories aren't fashionable these days."

His tone invited no comment.

"Before you meet my father, let me review the relationship between my father and yours. I'm sure you know about this but there are some things I'd like to add."

His face remained impassive, and his hands hung like dead things over the arms of his chair. It was just as well that he did not ask for confirmation that we knew about father's dealings with his agent. I was not sure what Josie knew, but I knew nothing.

"First of all, their relationship was a real one. You might ask what I mean by the word 'real'."

His pause was measured – long enough for us to consider his statement but too short to permit us to comment. I got the impression that the agent was repeating a well-used pitch which now slightly bored him.

"The relationship was more than just business," he said. "While business is what brought your father and my father together, the relationship was a long one, and both worked together toward a common goal. The goal was the development of Charles Saddler's career. His long-term ambitions were clear: to be famous and respected. This gave them a..."

"What has this got to do with us?" I asked.

A widening of the agent's eyes, and the pause which accompanied it, suggested that the agent disapproved of being interrupted.

"Our fathers had an arrangement that lasted nearly 40 years. They became good friends. Did you know that, even after your father had finished his writing career, he and my father would meet when Charles was in his London flat?"

I glanced at Josie. Her emails to me had become increasingly personal. While she was growing up, Charles Saddler had often been absent. Even when he was at home, she told me, he was not there. After the death of her mother in 1992, she said, he might just as well have moved out of the Ottermouth house altogether.

"The flat in London is news to me, yeah?"

"They had tea together most afternoons - in the Charing Cross Hotel."

His tone was entirely without comment and left me wondering whether or not the agent approved of the Charing Cross Hotel.

"Let me warn you," he said, "my father's friendship with Charles was of great importance to him. He knew everything about Charles, his aspirations as a writer and as a man. My father is loyal. Don't expect any revelations from him. Above all, I'd warn you not to pressurise. He's 90 years old, but he's on the ball and he speaks his mind. If he doesn't like you or your opinions, he'll kick you out, clear?"

When this introductory lecture was over, the agent stood up, opened the door behind him and ushered us into Peter Germaine's office. The door closed with a light click.

The small office was encased in books and sliced in two by a shaft of sunlight which came obliquely through a window and hit the floor by a desk. From the other side of the sunlight came the sounds of papers rustling, a nib scribbling and chair legs rubbing the carpet. A shadow rose and spread across the floor. Window blinds clattered and fell, and the shadow and the shaft of light were snuffed out. While my eyes adjusted to this change, a man's voice said:

"So, we meet again."

The voice was resonant and powered from the chest but the skin of his face and hands was so transparent he seemed intangible, a spirit draped in a black suit. The tired, hunting-dog eyes stirred my memory but it was the two vertical folds of skin dividing the forehead that finally revealed his identity to me. On this day, he had drawn the folds together in a way that suggested he was experiencing a headache.

"Perhaps, 'meet' is not the appropriate word," he said. "I'm sure you would..."

He stopped short as though he had come up against some internal blockage. For what seemed an age, I was aware only of the rise and fall of my chest and the distant roar of the London traffic. The old man looked older and frailer than the last time I had seen him wandering through the garden of remembrance.

"Yes," he said in answer to a question that had never been put. "It was the funeral."

Peter Germaine sat down, folded his hands and placed them on the top of the desk. His eyebrows were raised and a smile hovered over his cheeks.

"That was a time for saying goodbye to an old friend and not a time for making new ones."

He raised a shaking arm and pointed.

"You are Josie," he said.

He rolled his head sideways and looked at her along his arm as though it was the barrel of a rifle.

"Drawing attention to yourself with green hair? It's time you grew out of the habit."

The pointing finger swivelled to me. Germaine's

fingernails were broken and jagged.

"You are Nicholas, named with the purpose of reminding your father of his one and only muse."

Germaine watched my face for the effect of his words and said:

"Yes, we spend a lifetime trying to understand our fathers. We learn from them throughout our lives. When we think we have them in our hand, they slip away again and surprise us with something new."

Josie's hand alighted on my forearm, its fingers squeezing and comforting, and telling me to keep calm. To myself I said: "Fuck you, father." To Germaine, I said:

"Should I be flattered? Who was this muse – Nicole or Nicola? I know nothing about her. If father gave me my name for the purpose of reawakening his creative inspiration, it's not my problem."

In response, Germaine opened his hands and waved us to two chairs in front of his desk. While we took our seats, he said to the desktop:

"Until 2005, I knew your father very well. Yes, I wrote the obituary."

He raised his eyebrows but, as if we had communicated by some kind of telepathy, both Josie and I remained silent and still.

"I know most things about his life," Germaine said. "But nobody told me about his end. Can either of you enlighten me?"

I turned my head and looked at Josie. This was her territory. She gazed at her twiddling thumbs and then raised her hands and turned them over as though she were a conjuror revealing empty palms to an enchanted audience.

"From 2001, he rarely met anyone," she said. "He got kind of upset watching the news. This man, who made a living out of words, became monosyllabic. His life

143

gradually shut down in front of our eyes."

Germaine backed away slightly and fidgeted.

"And occasionally," he said, "memories which had lain dormant for 80 years would bubble up and he would talk about them, yes? But they were only fragments; random memories. Is it surprising that towards our end, our beginnings rise up to greet us again?"

I avoided the man's questioning eyes but Josie was undeterred by this gruff old man. She picked up the thread of his thoughts and ran with them.

"Not at all surprising," she said. "Dad went to the pool every morning and stood outside the baths. He smiled at the smell of chlorine and the distant splashing and disembodied cries of children. He said that those echoes were the very same echoes he'd heard when he was a boy. He said it was like listening to the past."

The old man bowed his head and slowly nodded. He appeared to consider making a comment but he emitted a light sigh and said:

"Go on."

"Some days," Josie said, "I went to the pool with him. He'd float on his back, his ears submerged, staring upwards while his arms worked like the blades of a windmill pushing him backwards. One day the lifeguard saw that the arms were no longer turning. Dad was lying with his head under the water. It was too late to save him. He'd been overcome."

"What did you feel?"

"I asked myself what was in his head when he died. Did he feel his life had been worthwhile? Was he thinking about his legacy? Was the world a better place because of him?"

The old man lifted his head.

"It's hardly likely. Charles was a good writer but he wasn't a great one. He knew that better than anyone. But I asked you what you felt, Josie."

Josie remained still. I almost heard her counting to ten before replying.

"A world was kind of lost to us with his death."

Germaine sat forward and placed his trembling hands together.

"Meaning?"

"He rarely talked about his past. We know little or nothing about his youth."

The old man smiled.

"A fate that befalls most children," he said. "What you want to know about your father's life is in the obituary. You need to know where to look and how to read between its lines. Charles was a great friend. He confided in me many things he did not want his family to know."

By claiming possession of some special knowledge, Peter Germaine had kidnapped Charles Saddler and taken ownership of him. Josie's response was immediate. Anger pulled at her eyes and tightened her jaw but I fidgeted on my chair and let my fingers brush her hand as a signal of sympathy and support.

"Then, perhaps you could tell us how much of himself dad put into his books, yeah?"

"His books were not about him but they could only have been written by him. Themes run through his crime novels and short stories; loneliness of existence, lost or eccentric people and how others react to difference. Many short stories deal with an absent parent. Yes, this subject has its origin in Charles' life."

The pitch of his voice rose on the word "life." It implied that Germaine was asking us for confirmation of an assumption but both Josie and I remained silent.

"He was sent to school in England when he was eight. He didn't see his father again. I often asked him the question you've asked me. How much of his work was autobiographical? He said his life wasn't interesting.

He claimed that he could invent more interesting characters than base them on the people he'd known. No, that's not to say that his father was no use to him. Charles made considerable fictional use of his father."

A moment of stillness followed this statement. From the corner of my eye, I saw that Josie had not flinched and she met Germaine's eyes with a concentrated stare of her own. She said:

"*The White Mountain* is dedicated to someone known simply as N. Do we know who she was?"

"We do," Germaine said.

"Nick was named after her, yeah? Can you tell us who she was?"

"No, I cannot."

Josie moved forward in her chair. Her eyes were poised for an angry outburst but she lifted her bag from the floor, rummaged inside it and pulled out a casket. Leaning forward, she placed it on the desk.

"We found this," she said.

Germaine stared at the casket for several seconds before taking it in both hands.

"There's a note inside it, yeah?"

The old man opened the box in a manner that suggested he was handling a recently discovered first edition of some favourite book. I stared in silence, faintly aware of the roar of traffic round Russell square and the world beyond it.

"Where did you find it?"

"In dad's office."

The old man picked out the card and scanned it. I wanted to break in and announce my presence by telling him that the quotation he was about to read was from the *Rubaiyat* of Omar Khayyam. But his attention was elsewhere. Nodding to himself, he was reading the verse under his breath as though it was a prayer.

"The end of the affair will be your departure," he

read. "It is a dream I will dream all my life."

"She – N – was very important to dad, yeah?"

The old man looked up.

"Don't make assumptions."

The folds of skin on his forehead drew together but Josie leaned forward and rested her elbows on Germaine's desk. Without taking her eyes from his, she smiled and said:

"You've kind of lost me."

Germaine looked at Josie with a steady but expressionless gaze.

"You father urged me never to betray this individual's identity and I swore I never would."

The blankness of his stare discouraged argument but Josie sat back in her chair, and, lowering her head, she met his blankness head on.

"And we received a cool wreath soon after dad's death. It was a wreath made of alpine plants and it came with an envelope containing edelweiss and a card with..."

"A photograph of a mountain in Germany and a quote from the *Rubaiyat*? It probably came from New York," Germaine said to the air around him.

Josie watched him carefully and, with admirable restraint, she nestled her cheek in the palm of her hand.

"So, you know who sent the wreath."

"It was certainly sent by N," Germaine said, "or on N's behalf and at N's request should N die before Charles."

Josie shook her head.

"Sorry," she said, "I can't get my head around that."

"N must have arranged it all. Dead or alive, N wanted the wreath, the edelweiss and the quotation to be present on the occasion of Charles' funeral."

Josie mumbled something into the palm of her hand but her words were rendered mute by the shriek of a siren from the world outside the window. Before she could repeat it, Germaine said:

"And your father must have arranged for his own funeral celebration, yes?"

"We kind of had no choice...."

"Nobody is blaming you," Germaine said. "Neither of you could've known what those songs meant to Charles. There's a symmetry about it all. He would've loved it."

Josie looked at him askance.

"You've kind of lost me again."

"The appearance of the wreath, the edelweiss and the verses from the *Rubaiyat* bring the story to a close."

"Story?"

"About the happiest and the most traumatic days of your father's life. And the songs Charles chose? They were the soundtrack to this story."

The period of calm which followed this assertion was my opportunity to remind the other two of my presence.

"You mean 'Somewhere over the Rainbow'?" I muttered, "I don't remember..."

"It was '*Komm Zuruck*' actually. Both songs were very popular when your father visited Germany in 1939."

Another question was poised on my lips but Josie was ahead of me.

"What happened in Germany that was so traumatic?"

Suddenly energised, the old man raised his arms and with a sweeping arc he indicated the books that surrounded us.

"It's all in his books," he said. "Especially *The White Mountain*."

"Can you clarify?"

"His first book was a purging experience for him."

"And it took him 20 years to write, yeah?"

Germaine made a swiping movement with one hand.

"That's all marketing stuff and nonsense," he said. "He finished the first draft within a year. He rewrote it several times after returning to *Oberwald*. He needed people to die, time to pass and history to settle before he felt safe. Should he publish and share what he knew with the world? Should he leave the past alone and let sleeping dogs lie? There are passages in *The White Mountain* in which you feel your father's anguish."

"For example?"

"The description of the body in a glacier. Sergio's discussions with the priest are also revealing. You can sense Sergio's agony. But that agony belongs to your father. What happened in 1939 influenced almost everything he wrote. It's even responsible for this last story you found and the fact that it ends where it does."

"I'm afraid you've kind of lost me again."

Germaine allowed his eyes to settle on some point behind us. His lips were parted and quivering. He drew out a handkerchief and wiped at his lips.

"Yes, the unfinished piece was written in 1991 but it was the penultimate chapter of a story which began in 1939."

Josie did not comment immediately. She seemed distant and gave nothing away - not even an indication that she was interested in hearing a response to her next question.

"So, it's autobiographical, yeah?"

"Yes and no. Charles inherited a lot of money on N's death. This is reflected in the story here."

He put his hand over the foolscap paper to emphasise which story he was talking about.

"Yes, it was a surprise, a bolt out of the blue, really. Until the day he received the letter from a New York solicitor, Charles believed that N had died in the war. That too is reflected in the story."

Josie removed her chin from the palm of her hand

and, leaning back in her chair, she crossed her legs.

"Did dad never make enquiries as to N's whereabouts?"

"I can't say. I do know that Charles was used to bereavement. His upbringing meant that it was a normal state of affairs. He didn't like it but he expected it and was comfortable with it. He never questioned it."

"What about N? She must've known father was alive. Why didn't she reach out and make contact?"

Germaine remained still and his eyes were steady and appraising.

"Perhaps the answer lies on this card," he said. "N wrote this for your father in 1939. 'The end of the affair will be your departure. It is a dream I will dream all my life.' And maybe that was how N wanted it to stay – a commitment to a dream."

Josie was suddenly snatched from us. Her face remained still but her eyes had drifted as if someone had called out to her from a place far away. I took the opportunity her silence gave me to jump in with a more mundane question.

"Why is it that both *The White Mountain* and his last story are set in Italy?"

The old man shook his head in a way that suggested he had eaten something too sour.

"Like most authors, Charles used his experiences creatively. If you decide to look for him in his books, you must remember this. Charles wrote and rewrote *The White Mountain* several times. In the end, he used his extensive knowledge of the Italian mountains and set the book there. The setting isn't important. Writers sometimes need to cover their own tracks."

"I'm sorry?"

"I have already told you. Charles waited until the early sixties before publishing his novel. He was afraid that by telling his version of events the past would come back to bite him."

"Was *The White Mountain* about his visit to Germany
– to *Oberwald*?"

A shadow fell over Germaine's face. The need for
politeness with me vanished completely and with no
attempt to conceal his impatience, he said:

"You really don't listen, do you?"

From the corner of my eye I saw Josie stir. She
appeared to be gathering herself for one last push. I saw
it in the thrust of her chin and heard it in her voice.

"Cool. So, are there any similarities between
*Oberwald* and the village in the novel?"

"You mean *Quero Vas*? Read *The White Mountain*.
You'll see the two main characters in a grave garden
outside *Quero Vas* and on a place called *Monte Croce*.
This translates into German as *Kreuzberg*. Visit this
mountain. You'll find traces of *Monte Croce* on it.
While you're there, look at the names of the memorial."

"Which memorial?" Josie asked.

"To the victims of Fascism."

She nodded but she was no longer listening and had
retreated to her faraway place.

"Do you know why he went to Germany in the first
place?" I asked.

Germaine's eyes darted from side to side.

"He went there for the same reasons that you are here
today," he said. "You think you're interested in Charles
Saddler, yes? But I'd say you are more interested in
yourself. As you are now a father, you find yourself
spending more time trying to understand your own father
so you can better relate to your own children. This is
quite normal. Now you are searching for answers to
questions about why your father did certain things in his
life, yes?"

My lips moved but I was unable to say anything.
Josie had returned to visit. She was studying the backs of

her hands and, in a tone that suggested she was thinking aloud, she said:

"We don't really know what he did."

Germaine looked at her with an expression on his face that suggested he was looking at a disobedient child.

"Look at what we do know," Germaine said. "When he went to Germany, he was nineteen. At the age of eight, he'd been removed from his family and sent to England. In many ways, he was an orphan. We have no evidence that Charles' father showed any interest in him whatsoever. What do you think he wanted?"

The emphasis on the word "you" emerged from his mouth like a challenge and he waited while the ghost of a smile played around his lips.

"A family?" Josie asked. "But why Germany?"

The old man looked at the two of us in turn. From outside came the sound of a passenger jet flying low over the city.

"Did he talk to either of you about it? Did you ever ask him?"

I answered with a quick shake of my head.

"I was too young," I said. "When he left, I was eight, and I..."

"And there'd been a kind of taboo around it when we were growing up. We dared not breach it, yeah?"

Germaine grimaced.

"Yes," he said. "Nicholas, you were made fatherless at the same age as Charles. You, Josie, were frustrated in your efforts to communicate through fear. Your father was prevented from communicating with his father through the absence of contact. And so, it goes on, yes? It travels from one generation to another. It becomes the norm. Why have you not had the guts to stand up and say 'Enough'?"

"Because, we..."

"That was a rhetorical question, Nicholas," Germaine said without moving. He looked tired, and the engine that powered his voice began to splutter. "Yes, there are other things you might like to know. Your father wanted his children to know him and to love him. Many of the events that shaped him are to be found in *The White Mountain.* It's up to you to find him and get to know him."

"You did know that dad wanted his ashes spread on the mountains in Germany, yeah?"

Germaine shuffled down in his chair, lowered his head and turned his face away as though he had been slapped. In a very thin voice, he said:

"On the 23 August, yes?"

The two folds of skin on his forehead drew together.

"On your way out, tell my son to come here."

Josie looked at me and made a movement of the head that suggested we should leave. While Josie notified the son of his father's orders, I held the door ajar and heard Germaine muttering: "Whatever you have done, you have to live with it. You have no choice because there is nothing else."

I was wondering whether these last words were directed at us in particular or at the world in general when the dark-suited son slipped behind me, strode over to the desk and stood at the old man's back as if he were his father's silhouette.

*

Before I left Josie at Russell Square tube station, I agreed that I would do my best to accompany her to *Oberwald* and scatter the ashes on 23 August. I watched her disappear through the ticket barrier and then turned back towards the square. The weather was closing in. I buttoned up my raincoat and turned into the wind that was blowing across the square. When I reached the steps of the School of Oriental and African Studies, I paused. Looking up and down the street, I pulled up the collar of my raincoat and took the steps two at a time. I made my way to the refectory and scanned the tables. A merry clatter emerged from the door and I saw Marie-Claude sitting alone at a table in the corner. She was occupied with some sort of paper and so I watched her from the entrance and wondered if I was going to have an affair with her. Until now, we had had a professional relationship – we were two of four other historians engaged with the notion that in order to have a new vision of the future it was necessary to have a new vision of the past.

I was not sure when this professional relationship turned into something with other possibilities. Perhaps the possibility had been there from the very beginning – from the first look or the first handshake and the touch of the skin. Perhaps we were insecure and setting up something that might act as an alternative should the need arise. Perhaps we were saying to our respective partners: *You can leave us if you like but we won't be caught napping.* I should have been reflecting on these possibilities and asking myself why I was chancing my marriage in this way. Instead, I found myself sitting in front of her and asking whether she was still going to the conference in Brighton that summer.

# 11

Outside the hut, the world is in motion. Birds and animals are foraging, and the water is flowing fast and slow, its rivulets carving gullies and tinkling through the melting snow. Inside the hut, a voice is whispering in my ear and reminding me I have no proof that *The White Mountain* is anything other than a work of fiction. Neither the words of an elderly literary agent nor the book itself constitute evidence to the contrary. Similarly, the investigations of an enthusiastic journalist hardly provide us with anything more than sensationalist headlines. Nobody will ever know how the victims of tyranny lying in the grave garden met their end. Stefan has lots of passion but he has no proof that the official version of events is a fabrication. What concerns me now, and has given rise to my fear of vengeance, is the other killing he mentioned – the killing that happened on 23 August 1939 - and Stefan told us about it just a couple of days ago on the evening of the riot.

\*

I glanced at my watch to signal to Josie that we had an appointment with Stefan. Getting up to leave, I told myself that Josie needed time to regain her composure. The truth was that I wanted some moments to reflect on why I had denied myself the purifying power of tears for so long. Making my way down the nave, I was sensitive to the eyes of the wooden Christ and of the unseen worshippers but I was also aware that revealing my emotional state to Josie had not resulted in the sense of personal debasement I had been expecting.

Since father's departure in 1960, keeping a tight rein on my inner life had been a personal trait I was proud of. Any welling emotion was hammered down. After a 50-year absence, tears reappeared at father's funeral. I would not say that this occasion opened the flood gates, but I barely batted an eyelid when tears fell again on coming face to face with my childhood pain just 10 days ago. On this August evening in *Oberwald*, I pushed through the church door and emerged in the open air feeling cleansed and resilient.

With detachment, I watched the crowds that were now filling the square and the street by the side of our hotel. The knots of men and women murmuring in the early evening light and gathering around me were objects of interest. Some were grouped together as people group together before a funeral, but larger groups were wandering *en masse* at the far end of the square, and their numbers were swelling.

One group in particular caught my attention. It had gathered by the hotel wall and a figure in black broke away from his fellows and slipped behind them. While the main body kicked their heels and stared at the ground, the black figure dived and rose with sweeping movements until, eventually, it melted back into the group. They marched off as one and left their protest as a theatrical symbol paint-sprayed on the hotel wall.

Between the frosted window and the street corner was a large swastika.

This procedure was repeated at the fountain. On this occasion, the person in black left the words, "Nazis out". The memorial to the mountain troops was also smeared with paint. Beyond this memorial, and along the road that led to the *Kreuzberg*, people were standing sentinel under the street lamps. They were holding their placards at arm's length and were as still as soldiers on parade. This allusion to things military was strengthened by the fact that they were all wearing black. The sturdiness of their placards suggested that these were protesters of substance and the hard-core activists I had noticed while standing at my room window.

Josie appeared beside me, and I took her arm. Despite the excitement that filled the air, she was composed and curious as to the identity of the people who had come to make their protest. I did not remember making one, but a decision had already been made and it was steering us round the church and towards the protesters on the *Kreuzberg* road.

In my peripheral vision, I glimpsed a shadow against the sky and heard a voice shouting to us in German. Josie tensed.

"Is that guy talking to us?"

I shook my head.

"He thinks we're someone else," I said.

When he shouted again, Josie's grip on my arm tightened.

"The guy is talking to us, yeah?"

We span round to face him. Standing on the memorial plinth and detached from the others, he was brandishing a can of paint and glaring at us. He shouted a third time. In response, I pointed vaguely towards the *Kreuzberg*. The shadow was having none of it. He grabbed at the memorial obelisk with one hand and, using his grip as a pivot, he swung round on his outstretched arm and stopped with his knees bent and his finger pointing at us. He shouted some more words, amongst which I heard the word "Nazi." A burst of almost maniacal laughter followed this outburst. Josie pulled at my arm.

"Let's move, yeah? Too much hate here."

We hurried on past the memorial and up the *Kreuzberg* road. Glancing over my shoulder, I saw the swelling mass of people between us and the hotel and, above them all, the man balanced like a court jester on the memorial plinth. His bitter cries followed us until he found another target.

Josie and I came to a halt at a comfortable distance from the street lamps. "Comfortable" meant far enough to avoid confrontation with the protesters and near enough to read the writing on the mounting boards. These boards were adorned with the names of places where, I supposed, the mountain troops had committed alleged crimes: *Komeno*, *Monte Grappa* and *Oberwald*. Josie and I inched forward to get a closer look at the boards dedicated to the four victims of tyranny. The names, Anton Beck, Joseph Dreher, Miriam Dornacher and Peter Weil, were written across them in black. Along the bottom of each board, and written in red, was the word "murder." Several boards displayed images of the victims. It was Miriam Dornacher's fine blond and curling hair that attracted us, and we crept towards her without suggestion or comment. We stared at the image for some time – perhaps meditating on the transience of beauty and youth – perhaps trying to articulate why the hair was so familiar.

There was not much time for reflection. Josie was playing with her fingers and her eyes began shifting from one hostile face to another. We strode back into the square and into the arms of the court jester. He had come down from his perch and was flitting around like a poisonous insect and infecting the crowd with bitterness. I tried steering Josie towards the hotel but the jester stood in front of us with his arms folded across his chest. I heard the shuffling feet of other protesters as they closed behind us. There was a muffled cry as someone kicked out, and a stone flew past my shins and landed with a crack against the church wall. I could think of nothing useful to say so I said:

"We're English."

"So - you're journalists," the jester said.

Josie untangled her arm from mine and thrust her face towards his.

"What's it to you?"

Her voice was drowned out when the mutterings behind us grew to shouts. I felt hot breath on the back of my neck and shoulders. The jester said:

"So, what are you going to write?"

Jostled from behind, Josie stumbled and an elbow poked my back. The jester unfolded his arms and indicated the hotel with a backward flick of his head.

"You know that the Nazi pigs are eating now in that hotel."

Beads of moisture broke out on my forehead. Someone shoved, and I heard Josie shouting:

"Back off, mate."

"These people are not welcome here," the jester said with a rise in his voice. "It is your duty to tell the world what they have done."

The jester was playing to the crowd and his statement was followed by a roar of approval.

"Crimes have been made in abroad and at home," he said. "These people have got away with murder."

Several protesters bellowed in anger.

"These meetings must be stopped."

Josie was pushed hard from behind and, as she

rocked forward on to the balls of her feet, another stone sped past and cracked against the wall. The jester raised a closed fist and shouted:

"*Edelweiss – Totenweiss. Gebirgsjaeger – Totenjaeger.*"

"Drama queen," Josie said, but her voice was lost as the crowd took up the chant and roared.

The jester smiled, waved his hand and then stepped sideways to allow us to pass. The crowd melted away but the chant continued in a deafening and familiar pattern that followed us past the fountain, to the bottom end of the square and into the side street that led to the hotel entrance. Only when I pushed through the glass doors did the chanting become a mere reverberation in my ear but any relief we felt faded with the line of men fanning out in front of us. Perhaps mistaking us for protesters, the men were blocking our way into the hotel.

Most of them were young men in grey tunics and caps with edelweiss on the left side. There were several older men in dark suits with rows of medals pinned to their lapels. They were all carrying what looked like collapsible black umbrellas. I had never imagined that the hotel manager's synthetic smile would appear as warm as it did. The man himself slapped me on the shoulder, took Josie's arm and beamed and smiled us into the bar. His barked order dispersed the umbrella men. He had clearly decided that the entrance porch to the hotel would be his battlefield, and he was going to defend it like Horatius at the bridge. He shrugged an apology at us.

"Just protecting our interests," he said.

In a place dominated by uniforms and designer gear, Stefan was conspicuous in his beret, his jeans and T-shirt. But as we threaded our way through the bar towards him, it was the activity in the square that drew my attention. Above Stefan's head, it was visible through the frosted glass window; a shadow play of human shapes dancing to the distant chant: *"Edelweiss – Totenweiss. Gebirgsjaeger – Totenjaeger."*

Stefan half-closed his laptop and stood up. The words, "Silence is argument carried out by other means," shouted at me from his T-shirt. He waved at me and then beamed at Josie, but she was uncommunicative, dropped into an armchair opposite the wall and refused to look at him. I saw her clasp her hands together and twiddle her thumbs while I turned a chair to face the entrance porch. If there was going to be trouble, I wanted to see it coming and see it I did through the window flanking the entrance porch. Trouble was developing in the passing heads, hats and placards that spilled over from the square and into our side street. I knew when they came close to the hotel entrance. Several uniformed men marched out of the function room and reinforced their comrades by the door. They stood in line beating their umbrellas on their open palms and tapping their feet in time to the sound of Glen Miller's "Moonlight Serenade."

If silence was argument carried out by other means, Josie was in full flow. Remaining mute, she had produced a pen from her bag and was rotating it between her fingers. I filled the silence with a rush of words. My attempts to make sense of our experiences in the square brought smiles from Stefan but when I described the jester, his smile dropped away, and he steadied his eyes on mine.

"The man is probably one of several plants," he said. "They're inserted by the police and will incite the crowd to violence. This gives the police the excuse to break the demonstration up."

He put his hand on the beret and shifted it around on his head.

"We might be in for fireworks."

I glanced a question at Josie, but she seemed

distracted and was assessing the world around her while the pen span.

"So, what about this other killing," I said.

"Assassination," Stefan said.

Josie raised her eyebrows as a signal of interest. She then replaced the pen in her bag, crossed her legs and watched the rise and fall of her swinging foot.

"Who was assassinated? I asked.

"I need to tell you a bit of local history," Stefan said to me.

Josie half-turned and looked with detached interest at the women hanging on to the arms of their partners. There was an unnatural atmosphere of peace and harmony around the bar but as the hotel grew more crowded, it became oppressive and hot, and a faint smell of perspiration filled the air. Stefan clicked his mouse several times and closed the laptop.

"So," he said. "I am sure you already know that in the1930s many opponents of the Nazi regime were either murdered or sent to the camps. That was as true for *Oberwald* as it was for other towns and regions in Germany. When the Nazi regime decided to hold the winter Olympics here in 1936 it was determined to present itself to the world as a friendly dictatorship. This was no easy task."

A blur of shadows moving against the frosted window caught my attention. There was an urgent whisper, then a voice called out, its tone commanding and strident and it was followed by the sound of running feet.

"*Oberwalders* had already made great strides in making life difficult for the Jews in this area. The Jewish language was forbidden and no Jew could buy or rent property in the towns in the region. Unfortunately for the organisers of the winter Olympics, *Oberwalders* were so enthusiastic in their anti-Semitic behaviour that it threatened to put the whole Olympic project in danger."

The hotel manager was hovering nearby and correcting the position of ashtrays or stroking away creases in tablecloths. He must have heard the sound of running feet when I did. He strode over to the soldiers at the doorway and said something to them. One of them marched to the function room and half-opened the door. Several more men emerged to the words of "Boogie woogie, here comes Suki." Joining the others at the entrance, they tapped their umbrellas to the musical beat. Stefan said:

"The fact was that anti-Jewish sentiment here had become so strong that organisers of the Olympics were concerned that anyone looking Jewish might be attacked during the event itself. As a result, all anti-Semitic signs were removed for the duration of the games."

The disembodied heads of several protesters moved past the oblong window. Their banners, swaying high above them, resembled sails in the wind. The soldiers at the door stiffened and then fanned out as the chanting began.

"*Edelweiss – Totenweiss. Gebirgsjaeger – Totenjaeger.*"

The guests leaned collectively sideways as if they were escaping a blast of hot air. Several women shot out of their seats and hurried towards the stairs.

"Organisers were not concerned for the safety of these Jewish people," Stefan said. "They were simply aware that the slightest disturbance in *Oberwald* would jeopardise the whole Olympic project. Remember, the winter games were essentially a dress-rehearsal for the summer games in Berlin. Any trouble with Jews in *Oberwald* and all the other competing nations might withdraw from the games in Berlin."

"*Edelweiss – Totenweiss. Gebirgsjaeger – Totenjaeger.*"

Perhaps encouraged by the arrival of darkness, the chant now had an aggressive edge that suggested the protesters were winding themselves up for a confrontation. There were more footfalls outside the frosted window and black-hooded heads passed by the window flanking the entrance. Above them, the sturdy banners, adorned with faces and names, prodded at the air. The soldiers merely rapped harder at their palms with their umbrellas.

"So," Stefan said, "you might ask, what happened after the games? For a while Jews were relatively safe here, but in time, the anti-Jewish signs were replaced, and the position of Jews became even more difficult than before. In June 1939, Franz Hackfeld became SS and Police Leader of this district. And, what were his orders?"

Over and above the chanting, I heard sirens wailing. The protesters must have heard it too. They began stamping their feet and, outside the hotel entrance, black-clothed figures had formed a phalanx. Those in the front row were stabbing at the glass doors with their sturdy placards.

"His orders were to make the region German again," Stefan said. "This news was enthusiastically received by the local towns and villages. During a previous posting he had proved himself as a ruthless officer prone to brutal and unscrupulous methods. He soon let it be known that he intended to rid this area of all Jews and all those with a Jewish heritage even if they had become Christian."

More lines of protesters joined the black phalanx at the door. The hotel manager occupied himself by correcting the table cloth on the table next to ours. The soldiers at the door calmly watched and gestured insults at the lines of black outside. Amongst the guests, hands reached for comforting hands while some of the men, anxious to be doing something, stood up and made calming gestures with their arms. The hotel manager urged them back to their seats and offered them something to drink.

"We know that a group of Jews was murdered on 16 August 1939. You have seen the memorial to them on the *Kreuzberg*. We don't know who was responsible. Did Hackfeld order the Alpine regiment to carry out these killings as a starter to what would follow?"

"You said the army denied any responsibility," I said.

"Given the regiment's record," Stefan said, "there's little doubt they would have carried out Hackfeld's orders. But the regiment has pointed out on many occasions that on the night the four Jews were murdered, the entire regiment was away in Austria. I have checked this claim and I found that indeed they were in Austria and flexing their muscles for the Third Reich."

Stefan glanced towards the glass doors and then, leaning forward, he gestured us to get close to him. His voice was low, conspiratorial and calm.

"So, the question remains, if the soldiers did not kill them, then who did?"

There was a rumbling sound like distant thunder. The black phalanx was pushing against the glass doors. Some of the guests made the sign of the cross but Josie folded her arms and, without removing her eyes from her foot, she said:

"Why don't you kind of tell us, yeah?"

"As I see it, there are only two other possibilities," Stefan said. "First, they committed suicide. This was not unknown amongst Jewish communities. But I interviewed someone years ago who told me the group died in a cellar after a number of grenades exploded amongst them. If they had killed themselves in this way, they would have found the pins. No pins were ever found."

Josie crossed and uncrossed her legs and exhaled with a sound that suggested she was losing her patience.

"And? Can you get to the point?"

"The only other possibility is that the townsfolk ..."

Josie interrupted with a shake of her head.

"Just so uncool. Tell us why the townspeople would kill their own?"

The sound of sirens grew louder while the young military men provoked the black phalanx with gestures that dared them to enter the hotel.

"We can only speculate," Stefan said. "Perhaps by killing four Jews, the townsfolk were demonstrating their loyalty to the regime. Perhaps the four young people were planning an assassination attempt of their own and the townsfolk were afraid of the reprisals that would follow."

Josie stuck her head forward and frowned into Stefan's silence.

"You're saying that we kind of don't know what happened, yeah?"

For the first time, Stefan seemed shaken and almost hurt. He retaliated with:

"Well, let me tell you something we are sure of."

At this point, a single protester broke through the glass doors and began chanting. The soldiers reacted to a man. They bundled him out of the door and threw him headlong into the street while one of the older men grabbed the banner, broke it over his thigh and threw it to the ground. I experienced a shock as if at a sudden noise. But it was not noise that had alarmed me. It was the sight of Miriam Dornacher's face staring at me from the floor.

"A week later, Hachfeld was spending the night in the refuge at the foot of the *Widderstein*. He was a keen mountaineer and walker. It was the evening of the 23 August 1939. At some point that night, he was shot dead by person or persons unknown."

He looked at me for a reaction but I was staring at the banner on the floor and struggling with a memory and its connection to the face of Miriam Dornacher. I heard Stefan as if from a place far away.

"Whether this was a revenge attack for the people killed the week before or a pre-emptive strike to stop more Jews from being killed is unclear. Perhaps the assassins were fulfilling the plans of those who were apparently murdered by the mountain troops the previous week. We simply do not know. What we do know is that at about this time most people with a Jewish history disappeared from the town. They probably escaped through Austria and thence to the US. To all intents and purposes, they simply disappeared from the face of the earth. What do you make of that?"

There was an aggressive edge to his question that contrasted with a lull in the protest while the phalanx gathered its strength. Still studying the rise and fall of her foot, Josie asked:

"Where can we find out about the victims? I mean, do we know anything about them?"

"The *Heimat* Museum – the town museum," Stefan said. "There is some information about who they were and how they died. Unsurprisingly, the museum gives us only the official version of events. They were killed by the soldiers on the orders of Hackfeld."

"Do you recall anything about the girl?" I asked.

"Miriam Dornacher? According to the museum, she was the daughter of jeweller, Hans Dornacher. We are told that Hackfeld ordered her murder because the Dornacher family were prominent members of the *Oberwalder* Jewish community. There is only a passing mention of her brother, Nicholas. They say he was due to take over the family firm. Maybe he escaped with the others. If he stayed, he would've been sent to a camp along with Hans in 1939 or 1940."

"Has nobody questioned this official version," I asked.

"Why should they? Nobody here wants to reopen old wounds. Huge amounts of money are due to come here with the Alpine World Ski Championships next year and with the 2018 winter Olympics. The future of hotels like this one will be settled for many years to come. Re-examination of old crimes is not on anyone's agenda."

There was a rumble as the phalanx rose as one and crashed through the doorway and into the porch. But the protesters had chosen the wrong moment.

Police in riot gear were filing down the street and lining up in rows outside the hotel entrance. The men in the front row stood with their feet apart and with the left foot forward. They were holding batons at their hips. At a command, they grasped the batons with their free hands and took rapid steps forward into the porch. They then snapped their left arms straight out and pushed with their right hand to bring the striking end of the baton into the protesters. I watched some placards falter and twist sideways while others dropped from view altogether. The protesters tumbled forward in a concentrated mass and, under their own momentum, they fell towards the soldiers. They were waiting, umbrellas in hand.

At this point, the second line of police came into the entrance porch. They held their batons at chest level and horizontal to the ground. When they were within reach of their prey, they snapped both arms outwards and drove the hapless mass further forward. The last of the placards fell and, unable to move arm or leg, the protesters stumbled within range of the army men.

I tried to calm myself by reflecting that the word "truncheon" probably originated from the Latin word, *truncus* - a trunk, but I had never seen a truncheon like the one the soldiers were using. They flicked their collective wrists, and the objects I had assumed to be umbrellas extended into springy batons.

I was able to see police batons rise and fall on the arms and legs of the unfortunates at the back of the scrimmage. The soldiers went in with wrists flicking. This caused a whipping effect in their springy batons which gave them tremendous striking power. The air was at once foul with blood and cries of pain. I guessed that the tip of their batons contained something solid and heavy, something that could easily break both skin and bone. From the mass of protesters defenceless arms, hands and heads protruded. One protester had lost his balance and had fallen forward. Trapped in the concentration of people and with his arms locked behind him, he was unable to fall. The sight of the head was too much for one old man in civilian clothes. Snatching the baton from the hands of a soldier, he stepped forward and brought the baton across his chest to strike. I turned my head away, and one lady screamed out:

"Oh my God, he's killed him."

I turned around in time to see her falling in a dead faint. Nobody seemed to notice her. Several other women were on their feet and covering their mouths while the men led them towards the stairs. Some of the protesters were crawling away between arms and legs and trying to make their way to the glass doors. Some of them managed to avoid the police but most were rounded up and led away. There were splashes of blood and other bits of human matter on the walls of the porch.

No sooner was the porch empty than the manager was there with members of the kitchen staff and cleaning the walls. Within minutes, the only indication of a violent demonstration was the line of police at the door, their uniforms barely visible in the darkness.

Stefan shifted his eyes from the door back to us.

"What will you write about?" I said.

"You are witnessing it now," he said and nodded towards the porch. It was now sparkling and the items of furniture had been replaced. The manager was walking around and offering free drinks to the guests. The soldiers had disappeared and closed the door to the function room, and some guests were returning to the bar area – smiling and talking quietly.

"Silence is argument carried on by other means. Cover up will be the point of my article. Who did kill the victims on the *Kreuzberg* and why?"

I was only half listening. The memory I had been struggling with had revealed itself and its connection was made. The memory was of my father's photos, a woman's arm and the lock of hair resting on it. The connection was with the protesters' placards, the face of Miriam Dornacher and her fine blond and curling hair. After almost 50 years, the girl in my father's photos had an identity. This girl, to whose arm my childish fantasy had attached the face that bewitched both my father and his rival, Von Stoutenberg, was now known to me. She was Miriam Dornacher.

# 12

Towards the end of July, I received a mail from Josie.

Nick

Soooooooo sorry for my silence over the last 2 weeks but since our visit to Germaine, I've been overwhelmed with the new online venture. And I've been browsing *The White Mountain* again. I know dad and your mum met when they were in Italy but did your mother ever talk about their walks in the Dolomites? I'd like to know which places dad was writing about. I can see loads of his usual themes in this book but I don't see much of him in it. I guess we'll have to wait until we get to *Oberwald* before we get our heads around the book. The passage about the discovery of the body in a glacier is weird. Have you read it? How do you think his "girl back home" would feel if, 45 years later, she saw the body of her beloved at the bottom of the glacier? Sooooo scary. Is it a warning about not messing around with the past?

At last, Miriam and I are coming to the end of sorting out dad's things. There are so many other things to do! The house is on the market, and Miriam is busy house-hunting. As for me, deadlines never cease! Anyway, there are only a few boxes left to sort through.

Btw –I can get a week off around the 23 August. You part-time academics at the uni also have August off, right? Have you decided yet? Can you come with me to Germany to do the ashes thing on 23 August? Come on, Nick. It'd be really cool! We should be no more than three days away.

Must dash.

Love

Josie

I opened my diary, checked the dates of the summer conference in Brighton and sent a non-committal mail to Marie-Claude.

Dear Marie Claude

Re: Meeting in Brighton, 26-30 August.

At the moment there is uncertainty about the date of the scattering of my father's ashes. I'll get back to you when I know for sure.

N

Josie's question about father's life in Italy was a reminder that I had not discussed it with my mother since I had been a child looking for that secret code in

*The White Mountain*. Nor had I visited her since May when I told her that father had died. At the time, she seemed unconcerned about it. In a sense, he had been dead to her for about 50 years, but you never know what people feel when a part of their past life goes away forever. My concern was that she had found too much time to dwell on his passing. This was my fault and I knew it. I always found excuses not to visit her, but the truth was that I did not want to face the consequences of mother's reflections.

When father left, my mother and I were fortunate that her job as a geography teacher gave her both time and money to spend on me. But mothers are not male role models and nor were her male companions. Most of these men showed no interest in me whatsoever. I was tolerated until I did something that upset my mother. Then the reprimands began, the fireworks started and my mother cried. Finally, the guilt, that I was somehow to blame, crept in. That guilt stayed with me in some shape or form until I reached adulthood. It would lie dormant for long periods, but in moments of crisis it flared up and told me that I was to blame for any nastiness that was occurring.

It had not been easy to put my mother in the care home. She had lived alone for years. In retrospect, I should have known something was wrong. Her memory had been failing for a long time. Her arithmetic skills went first, and I had taken care of her bills and her bank account. Living in another town, I used to look forward to her letters, but it got harder to read them and eventually they stopped altogether. When she called to tell me that an old boyfriend from the war was taking her to dinner, I knew something would have to be done.

Until the end of December 2008, I managed to take care of my mother at her home. This meant turning down good job opportunities. It also meant that my absence put a strain on my marriage. Liz told me that my priorities should lie with our family. But I was expecting more support from my wife and, from that time on, my attitude towards her changed. She simply was not what I had imagined her to be. It was during this period that Marie-Claude joined the department and, over innumerable coffees, I unburdened myself and found a sympathetic ear.

One day, the police called from mother's house and said she had telephoned them because she thought someone was hiding under her bed. I put my mother in a nursing home on the day after Christmas, 2008. She seemed unaware of what was going on that day. The Home Health aide came to give her a bath as usual, and then I told her it was time to go. My mother got up from her chair and went with me, not even asking where we were going. She was smiling as we entered the nursing home. I stayed with her all afternoon and most of that night.

The first few days went smoothly. But by the end of her first week in the nursing home, my mother fell ill. She was diagnosed with pneumonia and hospitalised. The doctor even asked me if she had made a will. After a week, she recovered and went back to the nursing home. She was never quite as responsive as before. Some of the time, she hardly knew I was there. But on the good days, she was alert and smiling. When I summoned up the courage to visit her at the end of July, it was one of the good days.

"Your father was English to the core, dear."

"What do you mean, mum?"

"When we lived in Italy, he reacted to everything in an English way – including the weather."

"What did he do?"

"Every time the sun shone, he said we simply had to go out and make the most of it."

"I see."

"I doubt it, dear. We spent far too much time outdoors."

"What else can you remember about him, mum?"

Your father was not a bad man," she said. "He just lost his way."

"How do you mean?"

"How could he do what he did to a young child? It broke my heart to see you, dear. Holding that book of his to your heart and idolising the man who left you. And he never even paid us maintenance, you know? Didn't I tell you?"

"I didn't know."

"I wrote to him and asked him about it."

"What did he say?"

"Nothing."

"Nothing?"

"He didn't reply."

"That's not good, mum."

"I think she must have hijacked his letters and opened them because I got a reply from her."

"His second wife, you mean? Maybe he gave her these things to deal with," I said in defence of my father.

"She was a bitch," my mother said and she said it without any trace of bitterness so that I believed her. "She asked me how I dared ask for money when I had so obviously failed in other ways."

"Didn't you write again?"

"I decided to let her find out for herself what sort of man he was."

"What sort of man was that, mum?"

"A man who didn't like women so much, dear."

According to the nurse, my mother had problems recalling the immediate past, but her long-term memory was resistant to the effects of her illness and, therefore, intact. I decided to tap into it by asking a question about the past.

"How did you meet him, mum?"

"We met when we were teaching in Verona," she said. "He asked me to marry him."

My beaming face encouraged her to tell me the summer-night story I had heard so many times before. They had been sitting at one of the tables that skirted Piazza Bra. The tables separated the bars and the shops from the fashionable people who appeared every evening for their stroll. My mother had been so absorbed in the well-rehearsed games of cat and mouse played out by the young men and women in front of her that she had not immediately noticed the ring lying next to the coffee cup.

"Tell me again about the walks in the mountains, mum."

"Oh yes. They were the good times."

"Where did you go?"

She lifted her hands as though to cup her face and opened her eyes wide. The combination of language and acting skills to animate unknown places had once made my mother's geography lessons very popular.

"Dark and forbidding places," she said. "Places which were full of ghosts."

She was staring over my shoulder and remembering.

"There was a huge memorial on one mountain," she said. "The sun gilded the distant peaks, which looked like islands rising from the sea. The valleys were already deep in shadow. The air was chill, and a silence and peace fell over the mountain. The world below ceased to exist. There were only the mountains, mists, and meadows, clouds and sky, golden light and the spirits of those who rested in this hallowed ground."

"Did he write that?"

"No, dear. I am telling you what I remember."

"Where was that mountain, mum?"

"Your father went walking there every day. I think he was looking for something. One day he came back and said we were leaving. No explanation – nothing. I think he had found what he wanted."

"Do you recall which mountain it was?"

"Of course, dear. It was *Monte Grappa*."

"Where's *Monte Grappa*, mum?"

"Above *Crespano del Grappa*, dear. On a clear day, you saw Venice in the distance and the sun sparkling on the Adriatic Sea."

"Would you like some tea?"

"One day, we met a most interesting couple," she said.

I thought I had lost her. She was going to tell me about one of those cocktail parties they had been obliged to attend in Verona.

"It was on, or near, *Monte Grappa*," she said. "Two Italians from the south had opened a refuge for walkers."

She looked closely into my eyes for a reaction. Then she said:

"And they did it in defiance of the CAI, the *Club Alpino Italiano*."

I think she was expecting me to be impressed. I was, but not by the defiance or by the prestige of the CAI. I had never heard my mother speak Italian. The way she reeled it off now was impressive.

"These southerners were convinced that their application had been turned down because of prejudice. They were probably right. They built a wooden shack and used their mule to bring up the food and drink. And they did it within sight of the official refuge. The owner was furious but what could he do?"

Eventually it was time to go. She asked:

"How's Mary?"

"She's fine," I said.

"Give her my love."

"I will," I said. But I knew I wouldn't. I had not seen my first wife for years.

That evening I reported back to Josie.

Dear Josie

Just back from visiting my mother. She told me things that confirm what Germaine told us. Mum said that when she and my father were in Verona, they often walked in the pre-Alpine region – just north of the city. She recalled places with dark atmospheres but she only named one place: *Monte Grappa*. She described it poetically. It must have made a great impression on her.

My guess is that our father put together the location for *The White Mountain* from a variety of sources. If you Google the town of *Quero Vas*, you'll find it on the Veneto plain between Venice and *Calalzo* in the Dolomites. The Valley of Prisoners is on a mountain called *Monte Pasubio*. This rises between *Vicenza* and *Rovereto* and was a key point on the Italian front line in World War 1.

My mother said that once, while walking on *Monte Grappa*, they met a man and his wife who had opened up a refuge for walkers. This is clearly reflected in *The White Mountain* but I have no idea who Spilmbergo was based on. Perhaps he was just a product of our father's imagination.

By the way, I'd love to come to *Oberwald* and do the ashes thing.

Best for now

Nick

In the middle of August, I received the report from the genealogist and forwarded it to Josie.

> Dear Josie
> Please find attached the report from the genealogist. I would print it out and pour yourself a large gin and tonic before reading. You'll need it. Let me know your thoughts! A new chapter opens.
> Best
> Nick

The next day I received Josie's reply.

> Wow!!! How cool is that? Still in a state of excitement. And I can now get my head around a letter Miriam unearthed from the writing desk in THE holy of holies. I have scanned and attached it. It is a letter to dad dated 1948 from someone in Germany. Soooooooooooo exciting!! The writer mentions being with dad in *Oberwald* in 1939! The most annoying thing is that there is no sender address and the second page of the letter has disappeared. Miriam thinks that the address was probably written on the envelope (as they do on the continent) and the envelope was thrown away. How annoying is that! We can discuss when we meet.
> We also found a letter, dated 1991, from a firm of solicitors. It states that dad was named as the main beneficiary of a deceased client. Why did we never know

about this??? The solicitor adds that his client left instructions that a personal letter be sent to Charles Saddler and the letter was enclosed. Unfortunately, the letter is not amongst the papers found by Miriam. There are creepy echoes here of dad's last story and adds credibility to Germaine's claim that the story was based on facts.

Miriam also found a package in the bookcase. It was from dad and addressed to you but for some reason it was never sent – the stamp was not franked. There is too much to scan so I will send this by snail mail and it should reach you in a few days. This just isn't cool and I hope it doesn't upset you, Nick.

Must dash and take care of yourself.
Love
Josie

I opened the attachment. I felt my stomach tighten when I read my father's name and the familiarity the shortened form suggested. For most of my life he had been "that man" or "he" or "the man who never came to see you."

My dearest Charlie
I am very, very happy that I have found you. I have to tell you a lot, but you must excuse me when there are terrible mistakes in my letter, but I hadn't a chance to speak English for the last 8 or 9 years. Excuse me please this awful envelope, but we haven't any more, and we can't buy any. I put our address on the back.

First, I want to tell you how glad my wife and I are that you are still alive – you who did change the world with what you made in *Oberwald*. It was only by chance that I read a story of yours and now I am sending this letter to your agent so he can give it over to you. I hope you don't now hate the German people but after all I will not blame you if you did. If I get no reply from you, I'll know why. So many terrible things have happened.

My greatest wish is that we shall be family again and meet again someday. My Inge sends her regards to you, and wants me to tell you that she never has hated English people but she likes them, and she is trying to forget the past awful days.

My dear Charlie, I have to tell your German family is now only me. My two brothers were died in the war. Thomas was died on *Monte Grappa* in the fight against the Italian partisans in January 1944 and was buried on the mountain as he would want. There is a stone to him on the south side of the mountain. Klaus is missed in Russia and has no known grave. My mother was in Berlin. She had to suffer terribly. She was starving. I couldn't help her. We weren't allowed to drive to Berlin. She was terribly longing for me. My mother starved to death. That I will never forget. It haunts me night and day.

Charlie – I have lost all I had and I have no photos of yours. Please send me one, I would be very happy. And one thing. I want to tell you about that terrible night in *Oberwald*. The regiment had nothing to do with that. We were away in the mountains.

> Maybe your great friend, Nikki, can tell you
> about it but I don't know what happened to
> him. Can you...

I sat at my desk and squeezed my eyes tight shut. I was still for some time but then I swung into action. Running ahead of my thoughts, I clicked on to my scanned *Oberwald* photos. The three men in uniform, my father, the woman and the man in civilian clothes gradually revealed themselves on my screen. I stared at them and, for the first time, I saw that the soldiers had edelweiss on the collar of their uniforms and on the left side of a grey cap. I supposed they were mountain troops. One of these soldiers had written to my father. Another had died on *Monte Grappa*. Perhaps my father had looked for, and found, this memorial to his dead cousin as my mother suggested. They all seemed to be the same age as my father at the time, but looking for family traits was a bit like a father willing himself to find a likeness between him and his baby son.

*Maybe your great friend, Nikki, can tell you about it but I don't know what happened to him. Can you...*

My hand grabbed for the mouse. The cursor quivered and careered across the photograph, missing the start button and disappearing from the screen. I steadied the mouse and found the start button. The programme bar shot up to obscure the photo, and I clicked on to my inbox and opened a mail from Marie-Claude entitled: Have you decided on the conference yet?

I shook my head, closed the mail and stared at the computer screen and at the outline of my face. Maybe I was looking for my feelings there, but I saw only pools of darkness. I grabbed at the phone and punched in Robby's number. Neither of us had time for small talk and I got to the point immediately. I had to see him, I said, and we eventually made an appointment to meet just a few days before I was to fly to Germany.

I replaced the receiver, clicked on to Josie's mail and reopened the attached 1948 letter. I covered my eyes with my hands. Gradually, I spread my fingers and located the last sentence.

*Maybe your great friend, Nikki, can tell you about it but I don't know what happened to him.*

It was the last word that grabbed for my attention and it was associated with confusion, shock and betrayal.

One word.

*Him.*

# 13

My home office is a very long way from this cold and dark mountain hut, but in my mind's eye I can still see my hands covering my face and I get a sense of the confusion that rocked me. Germaine was right about fathers always surprising us with something new. My father continues to elude me, but I am now getting glimpses of his life-before-me and how that life has shaped mine.

I understand what Germaine meant when he said that writing *The White Mountain* was a purging experience for my father, but I don't feel at all responsible for what my father did before I was born. The man in the hut might think differently. I may be about to pay the price for my father's actions. I may be held to account for something over which I had no control.

I wonder if father was hinting at this in the part of the book Germaine suggested to us. I flick the book open and find the short passage he recommended. Sergio was depressed. Musing on his position in *Quero Vas*, he recalled the only time he felt needed, a time when he was obliged to consider his own responsibilities to the past.

The powerful and patriarchal presence of the owner reminded Sergio of his own position and his own failures. He felt ashamed. In *Quero Vas*, nobody needed him except, perhaps, people like Caterina Bertone. In the two years of his tour of duty he had been called out only twice to help climbers who had been injured. Once though, his name had appeared in the national press.

The previous summer, a walker had discovered what he thought was the outline of a body embedded in the ice near the foot of the glacier in a nearby valley. As a Neapolitan, glaciers did not form part of Sergio's world. He had always imagined them to be giant ice-cubes, clean and angular, and blue. The reality was different. The lower extremities were foul and damp, and the ice-cubes of his imagination were stained dark and slimy with mud and damaged rock. Further up the glacier, he had been amazed at the plethora of crevasses, and the giant ice-cube groaned and cracked beneath him.

They had chipped at the surface ice, and then stillness fell on the party. Preserved in ice for more than forty-five years was the body of an Italian soldier. They guessed he had fallen into a crevasse in 1917 or 1918 and was about to emerge, to haunt briefly and then to disintegrate in the air of the early 1960s. They found a letter written to his girl at home in Palermo. It was a fragment of feeling, frozen for more than forty years, a ghost of love lingering on the snowy wastes of a mountain.

They speculated. Perhaps this man still existed in the memory of an old woman. Signor Stefano said that the frozen body was her memory, for memory preserved as well as ice. They had considered making enquiries. If the lady were alive, she would be old and have a life behind her. Waiting for death, she would be content with this life and happy with her memories. Luciana questioned their right to tamper with memory. This frozen body was, she said, the ghost of someone's hopes and dreams, and it belonged to the past. Sergio looked and he listened, and the rest of the world was non-existent as though it had vanished without a whisper.

Movements from behind surprise me and I snap the book shut. There is a rustling sound as the other man rises and makes for the door. It takes time for him to shuffle under the three arches, up the wooden steps and through the entrance. Josie is also stirring. Seconds later, a match flares, logs crackle, and the primus stove hisses.

Time passes me by, and a breath of wind coming through the entrance makes me shiver. From outside comes the intermittent sound of an old man's urine hitting the ground. I stare through the window. A mist has come down again and settles over us. Through the mist, I just make out the man's jabbing elbows as he does up the fly of his long johns. From the back, he looks old and not at all the angry man he was last night when he helped me into the hut with Josie.

*

The man removed his white gloves, stepped forward and gazed at Josie's injuries. I heard him say:

"What was so important about today that it could not wait until tomorrow?"

His eyes never left her face while his hands and fingers probed her head and pressured her shoulders and back with pinpoint accuracy. He did not press for an answer to his question, and I guessed the soothing tone of his words was intended to reassure Josie.

"And if you could just remove your hat for me?"

To demonstrate his meaning, he pulled off his own woollen hat and unwound the linen scarves from his head. Released from its confinement, his thick, white hair lifted. Strands of it fell over his forehead and glowed in the flickering firelight. He picked up an old cloth and handed it to me.

"Collect some snow in this – for an ice-pack."

He looked at me while I hesitated.

"It's OK," he said, "I really am a doctor."

I backed out under the tarpaulin, hurried past the primus stove and the makeshift benches, up the rickety steps, and into daylight. I shivered as the chill wind caught my face and hair. The ridge we had negotiated gleamed with bone-breaking menace through a tear in the mist. It was clear that unless the weather changed, we would have to spend the night on the mountain. Somehow, we had to contact the hotel and let them know we were safe.

I scooped up some snow, stuffed it in the old cloth and turned. I was expecting to see the hut but the mist was a mantle that rose and fell in waves, and the hut was invisible. I remained still and waited while a light snow began falling on my shoulders. When the hut jumped out of the mist, I recoiled at the sight of something so unexpected. My memory told me that the hut was a neglected ruin from another time; but now, I saw a couple of flower baskets hanging at the entrance and a bunch of flowers lay on a bench beside the door. For the first time, I noticed the turmoil of mud breaking through the covering of snow. Only the rucksack, lying near a puddle by the front door, was familiar. The last time I had seen the rucksack, it had been on Josie's back. I skirted the puddle, picked up the rucksack and re-entered the hut.

I paused at the top of the steps. A smell of coffee now mingled with the odour of terminal dampness, and the oil lamp was now casting a moonlight glow over the table, a cup and a discarded spoon. On the other side of the moon, the doctor fussed around my sister. He had removed his storm jacket, and I watched his white hair circling Josie's head while he inspected her ears, eyes and nose. Josie was sitting up, holding a cup in one hand and rubbing her eyes. I walked under the three arches and past the makeshift tables and benches towards the fire. Without acknowledging my presence, the doctor snatched the cloth from my hand and said to Josie:

"And do you remember falling today?"

He bent over her and laid the cloth over a wound on her forehead.

"Do you remember why you are here?"

There was a rustle from the fireside chair and the muffled sound of Josie speaking into her palm.

"She has had a little bump," the doctor said. "And she probably has mild concussion. I have given her a pain killer but she needs to rest now. She will have a headache for some days and she might throw up."

He turned his head then and spoke directly to me.

"Where are you staying?"

When I told him, he pulled a mobile phone from his trouser pocket and punched at the keys. The conversation with our hotel manager was short and sharp but I understood nothing. The two men could have been talking about the weather. The doctor pocketed the phone and said:

"So – they know you are safe. When you get down to *Oberwald*, you had better have another doctor check her over."

A moment of stillness followed while the doctor studied my face.

"There's no need to be so alarmed," he said. "It's just as a precaution."

I smiled in an attempt to build some kind of connecting bridge to him but I might just as well have smiled into the darkness.

"You know," he said, "you are two times lucky today."

I raised questioning eyebrows.

"I was here quite by chance."

"And?"

"And - I am a doctor."

His English was fluent but his reluctance to run his words together and abbreviate them made his language clipped and pedantic.

There was a rustle from behind. Josie was sitting bolt upright.

"What's that sound?" she said.

She raised her hand to her ear but I heard nothing except the crackling of the fire and the drip-dripping from above. The piece of tarpaulin over our heads was stretched tight and bulging.

"What are we doing here?" Josie said.

The doctor swung round to address me.

"A good question," he said. "Why are you here? You have put all our lives in danger. I think you owe me an explanation."

My response was rendered incoherent by false starts

and hesitations, but Josie jumped to her feet and came to my rescue. Her face was full with the excitement of a sudden memory.

"The ashes," she said. "We're here to scatter his ashes, yeah? He kind of told us to do it on 23 August. It was his wish."

"He?"

Neither Josie nor I replied. Josie moved backwards and dropped down into her seat. Resting her elbow on the side table, she rubbed at her eyes again.

"The double vision will pass," the doctor said to Josie.

"How long will she need?" I asked.

The doctor put his hand on Josie's shoulder and let it rest there before turning to me.

"Try again, please," he said. "Who is 'he'?"

Something cracked. It was only a piece of burning wood in the grate but it broke the spell that had paralysed me.

"Our father," I said.

"So, you know why this was his wish?"

I expressed an apology with contortions of my face.

"No, we don't know, I'm afraid."

The doctor looked hurt.

"Unbelievable," he said.

He then turned to face Josie, placed his hands behind his back and stretched one leg out towards her. His head was tilted downwards and he was staring sideways as if he had heard someone whispering to him from behind. With a degree of gentleness that was absent when he addressed me, he said:

"And do you know why your dad wanted his ashes scattered here on the *Widderstein*?"

"He stipulated both the date and the place, yeah?"

"And you don't know why?"

"You got it."

"He must have known this place."

"We kind of know he was here in August 1939. He climbed the *Widderstein* with a friend."

"Did your father tell you this?"

"No, he never talked about it."

"Then how do you 'kind of know' he was here at all?"

"Things that turned up after he died. Dad's agent mentioned it too, yeah?"

"Agent?"

"Dad was a writer," Josie said. "He and his agent were close friends."

The doctor said nothing, and neither his face nor the tone of his voice had expressed the slightest interest in our answers. I wondered if he was simply engaging Josie in conversation in order to assess her mental state. But he surprised me with:

"Yes, it is one of the tragedies of life that when children become interested in their parents, both mother and father are no longer there. Then comes the regret, am I right? Do you feel guilty?"

"No," I said.

I looked down at Josie awaiting her response. She leaned her head against the chair back and shook her head.

"And what sort of things did your father write?"

"Our father was a novelist," I said.

"Novels? What sort of novels?"

"Crime fiction," I said.

The doctor spun round. His eyebrows were raised.

"Like your famous Sherlock Holmes?"

He seemed pleased that he could connect with me in this way and his pleasure brought the outline of a smile to his face.

"But not quite so popular," I said.

"Why not?"

I remained silent for a while, listening to the plip-plop of the dripping water, and wondering whether it might overflow - whether I was ready to let go of my old crutch, the perfect father.

"His books were a product of their time. By the seventies, they were old-fashioned."

"So – not the lasting appeal of Sir Arthur, then."

"Absolutely not."

I looked towards Josie. One side of her face was veiled in darkness. In contrast, the other side glowed in the firelight and there was an open expression in this bright eye which urged me to add:

"My father was not a great author."

The doctor said nothing and Josie bowed her head. It was an act of reverence in the face of something that had passed away. She looked up and added:

"He actually blamed the lack of sales on the sadness of his work."

"In a crime novel?" the doctor said, suddenly reanimated.

Josie nodded but the movement made her wince with pain. Rubbing at her forehead, she said:

"The characters in his books are often outsiders. His books reflect their loneliness. According to his agent, father wrote his first novel *The White Mountain*, as a purging experience."

"Purging? You must excuse me, but English is not my mother tongue."

Josie was losing her battle with the headache, but she squinted at the doctor and jumped in with:

"Purging? Yes, it's about removing the guilt we might feel."

"Guilt about what?"

"We don't know," I said. "The time distance is too great and the principal actors are all dead."

"But the novel must tell you something about his

guilt."

Josie came back with:

"If you can kind of separate fact from fiction that might be true."

"And have you separated fact from fiction?"

Josie peered at him through half-closed eyelids.

"What we can say is that the story takes place in Italy, but that its setting comes from a variety of locations, yeah?"

Josie was excited, her words were running together and some of them were incomprehensible.

"That's right," I said. "He wrote about a monument to the partisans on a place called *Monte Croce* and above a town called *Quero Vas*. But to all intents and purposes, he was writing about the monument on the *Kreuzberg* above a town called *Oberwald*."

"And what does the book say?"

"In the book, the monument is not what it seems to be," I said. "In the book, the partisans were not murdered by the Germans but by their own people."

"In the book?"

"Yes, in the book."

"And why did they do this? In the book, I mean."

"Some young villagers were planning partisan attacks on the German occupiers. Others weren't happy about this. They were afraid of the reprisals that would follow."

"Interesting. And does this crime fiction, as you call it, reflect reality?"

"I really can't say," I said.

There followed a silence and a clash of eye contact that forced me to avert my gaze.

"Father also writes about the shooting of a man in the mountains," I said.

"Who is that man?"

"In the book, he is called 'The German' – someone

who was planning bad things in the region."

"Perhaps...," the doctor began and then he allowed his thoughts to hang in the air as if unwilling to hear them spoken aloud. I did not attempt to break the silence that fell between us and focused on the plip plop from above. Eventually, he said:

"And your father was adamant that his ashes be scattered on 23 August?"

"Yes."

The doctor spun round and put his hands behind his back and his question to the wall.

"So why do you think he came to *Oberwald* in the first place – in 1939, I mean?"

The sudden, tilting movement of his head suggested that he was expecting a prompt answer to his question. I said:

"To meet his family, perhaps. He discovered he had relations in Germany and came over to meet them. And while he was here, we think he climbed the *Widderstein* with someone he befriended. Perhaps they even had a relationship. We don't know anything for sure."

"That is curious. It is also lucky for you."

"Why?"

"It was lucky for you he chose 23rd August. On any other day, this hut would have been empty. It is no longer used, you see?"

I nodded but it was clear that the thoughts of the doctor had drifted away to other things. He turned to Josie and grabbed at her hand.

"You need to sleep, young lady. But before you do, we must carry out your father's wishes while there is still some daylight."

I glanced through the window and saw that twilight was approaching through the mist. I walked over to my rucksack and drew out the urn while the doctor helped Josie into her cagoule. He was wrapping a scarf round her neck when I approached and said:

"Is it time?"

"It's time," Josie whispered.

I took the cloth cover from the top of the urn and nestled it in my hand. It was a plain earthenware pot but it was by no means plain what I was expected to do with it. The doctor and I guided Josie through the hut. The door knob rattled under my groping hand, and we entered the silence of the mist.

Josie walked ahead with the doctor while I remained at the door. I stared into the white world in front of me and for a moment, I was filled with the delight of solitude. I was a man about to be liberated from his past. I looked around, but seeing no sign of new beginnings, I set off in pursuit of Josie and the doctor.

We lined up in the mist and, checking the direction of the wind, I turned to Josie. She held out her hands bowl-like, and I poured some of the ashes into them.

"Try to remember the last time you saw him," I said, "in the fullness of himself."

Then I tossed the remaining ashes into the air. The dense sand-like matter fell to the ground but some of the ashes were of powder and became airborne. The white cloud that spread out in front of us merged with the mist and disappeared in a second.

"Will his memory kind of disappear so quickly?"

"He'll return in other ways," I said.

"Like?"

"A gentle memory; an unexpected presence, or perhaps in a shadow that appears at your feet."

I was not sure how long we stood reflecting in this manner but I suddenly sensed a look of goodbye in Josie's eyes. She took several deliberate steps forward, and flung her arms upwards.

"There you go, dad," she said.

She muttered something while the ashes disappeared

with the wind. She then turned, strode off in the direction of the hut and was swallowed up in the mist. No words came from beyond the white wall. There was neither a footfall nor a sound more until the refuge door opened and then slammed shut.

The doctor was sitting on his haunches, his hands on the earth, his head thrown back. He was looking towards the hidden sky when he said to nobody in particular:

"I need to say a few words for my father."

I then heard a few muttered lines, perhaps a prayer and it finished on a long and whispered note. With a slow but powerful push of his thighs, the doctor rose from the mud. He threw his arms wide open, held them suspended for some seconds and then let them fall uselessly by his side. It was a perfect gesture that communicated the inexpressible – man's impotence in the face of death.

"We can only take care of the living," he said. "But at least this spot now says, 'They were here. They lived a life.' This place is now sacred to their memory."

"Who are 'they'?" I said.

But he had already turned and was walking into the mist. I followed him into the hut and down towards the fire where Josie was sitting again. He was fussing around her and when he looked at me, I saw an expression on his face that suggested he was poised for a confrontation. He stepped away from Josie and pre-empted any question I might have.

"I am seventy-two," he said. "I have been coming here for 50 years on this day and in this month in order to celebrate my father's memory."

We exchanged a long and silent star. When he turned to Josie and covered her with a blanket, he said:

"I have spent my life healing. I shall continue to do so. Only sometimes, forgiveness is harder..."

I swear my voice was shaking when I asked:

"So – why do you come here to celebrate your father's memory?"

"I am tired now. I advise you to get some sleep, too. We shall have to go down in the morning."

"Please," I said, "why do you come to this place?"

I did not need to hear his explanation. It was all in *The White Mountain* after all. The book had been a purging experience.

"He died here in 1939."

*The person they had come to find was in the refuge that nestled in the shadow of a great peak.*

"Here? In this hut?"

*There was a metallic click as a cartridge was forced up by the clip's spring.*

"Not quite," the doctor said. "Outside on the terrace."

*Birds had taken to flight in a frenzy of beating wings but the warning came too late for the person who lay face down on the refuge terrace.*

"It was 23 August 1939," the doctor said.

*The hand was outstretched and his blood dripped and drenched the earth under him.*

"My father was shot dead on the terrace of this hut."

# 14

I've got some news," Robby said. "I'm sure you'll understand that..."

A double-decker bus with a faulty silencer roared away from the lights. Black plumes of smoke rose into the air as the bus growled past the Hotel Russell and polluted its way down Southampton Row. We were sitting under a sunshade in the Cafe in the Square, a middle point between Robby's college and mine. Luca, the Italian waiter, waltzed over to our table and slipped his order pad from a back pocket.

"*Prego, signori.*"

I tried to catch his eye but his head was hidden behind the rim of our sunshade. While he jotted down our order, his torso swivelled from the hip and I imagined his eyes seeking eyes, his ears alert to every sound. The cafe terrace was his domain, and he was performing on it, bathing in the attention of the women around him. He pocketed the order pad and, diving under the sunshade, he swept away the used crockery.

"*Grazie, signori,*" he said and danced away.

"And I've got some news about our family history," I

said to Robby. "You might be interested in it."

I glanced at him quickly, but he picked up his multi-coloured mobile phone and snuggled it into the palm of his hand. To me he was still a boy but I could see that his tight dark curls and light skin made him an attractive man. On this day, there was something reserved and reticent about him that made him look like a tight-lipped puritan.

Robby thumbed at his phone and, without looking up, he said:

"Your family history, dad? Really?"

"Yes, really."

"Where did you get this exciting news, dad?"

He swiped at his phone with his index finger and plunged into his electronic world. I leaned forward.

"The genealogist," I said on a rising tone.

"What did you find out, dad?"

I had the glint of a thought that Robby was not interested. Perhaps it was the falling tone of his question that made him sound indifferent.

"Charles Saddler's father, Peter, was born in Germany in 1895," I said.

My words startled me by their expectant and direct tone. I softened them a bit. "I mean, Peter's father was German and his mother was English."

"I see."

A slight sideways movement of Robby's face and a thinning of his lips suggested that indifference had become irritation. He was still gazing at his mobile phone when a presence at my back announced the return of Luca. He bowed under the perimeter of the sunshade, and our order clinked onto the table.

"*Prego, signori*," he said and swayed away without a sound.

I wanted to reach out and grab Robby by the shoulders and give him a good shake but I knew that if I did, he would slip through my hands like mist.

"Peter and his mother were in England when the First World War broke out," I said, aware of the impatience that had crept into my voice. "Their surname had a suspiciously Germanic sound to it. Apparently, Peter's mother divorced her German husband and changed the family name to something more English."

I hunched my shoulders and wrapped my hands around my coffee cup in order to feel its warmth.

"Our original name was Santner," I said.

"Well, we're Saddler now."

I looked down at the table top. My gaze was flitting from the cigarette burns to the peeling Formica edges when I told him that Peter's mother died of Spanish flu in 1919, and that Peter continued his career in the Indian army. I was looking at the water jet fountain in the middle of the square when I added:

"And my father - your grandfather - was born in India in 1920."

"Interesting."

I allowed my eyes to rest on the histrionic facade of the Hotel Russell before closing them for a moment. I guessed that all fathers were destined to disappoint their sons by failing to perform to a standard that was never meant to be. I suspected that, even though he was now an adult, Robby was still in the process of destroying his image of the perfect father. Finding only flaws and frailties in me, Robby might even grow angry at me for the loss. I supposed I could help this process by admitting my mistakes, apologising for wrongdoings, and declaring my limitations. At the same time, I could compliment Robby and point out those things he could do that I could not; but, perhaps, praise was what wives and friends were supposed to give. I somehow did not expect Robby to take compliments from me. Anyway, I could not bring myself to give them.

When I opened my eyes again, I saw two familiar girls sitting on the edge of the terrace. Young, leggy and highly efficient, Jo and Jilly were admin assistants from Marie Claude's departmental office. I had once fallen foul of them by questioning them about my teaching timetable.

"We don't do timetables," Jilly had said.

Neither of them forgot my testy response. Unfortunately, Jo and Jilly were seriously plugged in to the faculty grapevine and both actively contributed to its efficiency.

I lowered the tone of my voice.

"My grandfather, Peter, had a brother named Udo."

I watched Jo and Jilly in my peripheral vision. They were giggling and conversing in closed whispers. They were sure to know about my impending affair, and I had no trouble imagining the gist of their conversation. Illicit faculty relationships were their bread and butter.

"Men always go for perfection," Jo would be saying.

I could almost hear Jilly's reply.

"And too late they find out that the perfect woman doesn't exist."

Robby was taking in everything around him. He directed a long smiling look at an attractive jogger making her way round the perimeter track. She returned his gaze with an equally smiling moment. I was pleased at this show of feeling. It was an overt sign that Robby was human. My pleasure came with a sense of concern. Robby had been married for only 3 years. Like most fathers, I wished my son happiness. I also wished him a degree of marital contentment.

"I never met your father," Robby said. "And as far as I'm aware, you hardly knew him either."

"You're right," I said, my voice edged with discomfort.

Robby leaned back in his chair, shook his head and

folded his arms tight to his chest. His abrupt stillness suggested to me that his mood had darkened.

"Why is all this so important to you, dad?"

The bitter tone with which Robby asked the question confirmed my assumption that we had disconnected and I was in for a grilling.

"Because if my great uncle Udo had children," I said, "perhaps my father went to Germany in 1939 to visit them."

"Didn't know he was in Germany in 1939."

I reached into my briefcase and rummaged around for the packet of father's photos. Jo and Jilly were looking at me and nudging each other. As I pulled the photos from my bag, I asked myself if this was how it would be. Reduced to a nudge and a knowing wink, I would become the faculty figure of fun who had left his wife and child in tears.

"Look at these," I said.

Carefully avoiding the cigarette burns and the peeling Formica, I laid out the photos in rows of three.

"Maybe the boys in the photos are the family – his cousins."

Robby leaned forward and, head down, he rested his folded arms on the table top. To give him credit, Robby did more than just glance at the pictures. He studied them with the interest he would show on reading any original text. This interest encouraged me, and I gave him a commentary that followed the path of his eyes.

"That's my father. These men in uniform are his cousins. The man and the woman are people he befriended in *Oberwald*."

Robby's nods encouraged me still further and I was about to tell him about the annotations on the back when Robby interrupted with:

"You're slipping, dad. Do you call this evidence?"

I held my tongue, counted to three and pulled the

1948 letter from my briefcase. I held the letter under his nose, suggested that he read it and slapped it down on the table.

"Try that," I said.

Robby read the letter with the same detached interest with which he had studied the photos.

"You know as well as I do, dad, that this letter and the photos do not constitute evidence. Of course, you can believe what you want to believe but I'd call it wishful thinking."

Luca passed by our table, brushed the sunshade and sent it spinning.

"Did you ever read *The White Mountain*?" I said.

Robby drew back from the table and looked obliquely at the table top. He nodded.

"Long time ago. It's very much a product of its time, you know? After-the-war guilt and all that."

"Father's former agent told us he was writing about something that happened to my father when he was in *Oberwald*."

"How on earth does he know that, dad?"

An electronic version of *The William Tell Overture* sounded. Robby swiped at the phone and lifted it to his ear. He jumped to his feet, pointed at the phone and mouthed:

"It's Pam."

I made a heart sign with my hands but before I could signal that he should give it to his wife, Robby turned his back and walked away. He came to a halt on the grass verge just behind Jo and Jilly. I looked at Robby out of the corner of an eye. He was holding the phone close to his ear and kicking at something real or imaginary by his feet. This show of feeling did not disturb the two girls. Their conversation was punctuated with smiles and laughter and barely disguised glances in my direction. It was easy to imagine their conversation.

"Saddler is still a boy."

"Still looking for the perfect father."

"Plonker."

"And he judges everyone accordingly - including women."

"Who does he think he is? Prince Charming?"

"He might just as well be looking for Sleeping Beauty."

Robby took another vicious kick at some object at his feet. I watched him pocket the phone and sidle away from Marie-Claude's colleagues. He shuffled through the tables and sunshades and eventually came back and sat down. He put the phone in front of him.

"Everything OK," I asked.

Robby just stared at me. I directed him back to the photos.

"Do you see a family likeness here," I said.

Robby shook his head.

"He even instructed that his ashes be spread on the mountains here."

"Where?"

"In *Oberwald.*"

"Why, dad? Do you know why?"

I spread my hands.

"It was in his will. The place and the date were clearly stipulated. Father wanted his ashes scattered above *Oberwald*, on the *Widderstein* and on 23 August."

"In a few days, then? Do you know why *Oberwald* and this particular mountain are significant?"

I told Robby how my father and N had exchanged edelweiss and quotations from the *Rubaiyat* when my father left *Oberwald* in 1939.

"They were expressions of eternal love and affection and they turned up again 70 years later. Father's gift to N turned up at his funeral. N's gift to father was found in his office after his death."

"How romantic is that?"

"Didn't you notice," I said, aware that the irritation in my voice had returned, "that the 1948 letter makes it clear that N was a man?"

Robby shook his head again.

"You know, dad, your father's books are concerned with the powerless and with people who are somehow different. No doubt, he saw himself in the same light. It would be no surprise, would it, dad? Homosexuality was illegal in the UK until 1967. In a sense, he was a loner and a victim of repression. But what interests me, dad, is how you feel about it. Is it too much for you that your father might have been gay?"

His challenge stopped me in my tracks but it was the inferred criticism that came with it that obliged me to count to five before considering a reply. I had always seen myself as a product of sixties liberalism but I had never really considered what life had been like for gay men until homosexuality was decriminalised in 1967. Perhaps it was not father's gayness that bothered me but the fact that I had spent my life thinking he was straight. At no time in my life, from my childhood fantasies of the hut with no name to the appearance of the enigmatic N, had it occurred to me that father might have been writing about gay relationships.

"So, dad, how close were you to your father when a secret as big as this was kept from you? And think of the effort it took to keep it hidden from his wives and children."

Robby was right. What must life have been like for the son of an Indian army officer in a world that could imprison you for 2 years with hard labour? The threat of exposure and disgrace must have hung over him like a cloud. I knew that Britain in the fifties was gripped by a fear of homosexuality. Some of Britain and America's most prized diplomats and scientists, including Guy

Burgess and Donald Maclean, were exposed not only as traitors but as homosexuals. Robby had scored a point against me, but I was damned if was going to let him win this argument.

"His homosexuality doesn't bother me in the least."

For the first time, a smile appeared on Robby's face.

"Dad, it really doesn't matter what you think about homosexuality, does it? Your father was remarkable by his absence and not by his sexuality. It's too late to change that and any damage it caused. Please, dad, don't try to repair the damage he did by projecting it on to me. OK?"

I am not sure what Robby said after that. Luca had arrived at Jo and Jilly's table and his head was well inside the rim of their umbrella. With one hand on his hip, the other clasped Jo's arm and helped her to her feet. They stood toe to toe for a moment, before Luca proffered his hand to Jilly. Both girls were all fidget and fluster, their giggles intended for Luca's ears and not for mine. I stared at them both, my face as expressionless as I could make it but my mind was running off on its own. Jo and Jilly had never been looking at me at all.

I sensed even before I had thought it through that it was my own inner voices I had been listening to. My father was indeed remarkable only by his absence and I had never been able to go through the process of paternal downsizing and form an adult relationship with his memory.

Robby was searching my eyes, but I had drifted away to another place. I looked at my watch as a signal that I had to go.

"Meeting with a colleague," I said.

For the first time that afternoon, I saw a shadow of doubt in Robby's eyes.

"Before you go, can I speak to you, dad? I need your help."

"No time now," I said. "Give me a ring."

I left him then and, in order to avoid Jo and Jilly, I headed for a gap in the sunshades on the hotel-side of the square. I did not turn and give one final wave to Robby. I was concerned about the girls. If our eyes met, they would read the signs on my face and in my eyes that told them: *Yes, what I heard you say is true.*

I spent the rest of the afternoon working with a colleague on the preparation of a paper for the Brighton conference. We felt that, in a world that was living in a permanent present, we needed to make a case for history. We argued that much of what people did, felt and thought was governed by history. Understanding these influences was a necessity if we were to free ourselves and become someone different. Essentially, we were suggesting that it was possible for all of us to form fresh views of our personal histories and, consequently, to break away from the values we were brought up with and choose our own.

When I got home that evening, I went straight to my office and mailed Marie-Claude. I felt that the future success or failure of my marriage was hanging on a thread.

Dear Marie Claude
Still unsure as to the date of the ashes.
I'll be in touch. N

Liz had already picked up my post and placed it next to my computer. The package Josie had mentioned in her mail was waiting for me. I sliced it open. There was a bundle of papers inside and a brief note from my father to me and dated 1963. It read:

"Another Black Patch story for you. If you like it let me know and I'll write you another. Love Dad."

I picked up the note and the brown paper envelope,

which contained the story. I then went to the bookcase and took out my copy of *The White Mountain*. I sat down at my desk and took the story out of its envelope. I placed the open book on my lap and laid the letter and the Black Patch manuscript on top of it.

Time stood still.

I let my fingertips run over my father's neat, right-slanted handwriting and allowed them to pause in the characteristic gaps between the letters. Then, I laid both hands palms downwards on the letter. For a while, I meditated on the word "pain" and whether it was somehow related to the words "penal," "penance" and "penalty."

I closed my eyes and remained still.

I sat like that for a long time.

# 15

The doctor emerges through whirls in the mist and heads for the entrance to the hut. The doorknob rattles, the door clicks shut and the man's feet clatter down the steps. Through the air, thick with dust, his voice reaches out to us.

"The weather will get better today. We can go down together."

Josie is spooning coffee into plastic beakers. She has a woollen hat on her head, and her cheeks, caught in the leap of the flames, are glowing. The muscles of her jaw ripple and her bottom lip trembles as though she is reluctant to release the words that balance on it.

"What has happened here?"

The doctor passes the cables, the graffiti and the tarpaulin sheet and appears by Josie's side.

"Don't you remember what happened yesterday?"

Josie shakes her head and bites at her bottom lip.

"You fell on the ridge," he says.

She leans forward and scratches at the bare brickwork with her nail. Powdery dust falls to the floor.

"I kind of remember scattering his ashes, yeah?"

One eye glistens brightly in the light of the fire, and a red tear runs down her cheek.

"I expect I'll remember the fall one day. It'll kind of come to me without warning, yeah?"

Josie and the doctor exchange a glance and, for a moment, only the sound of the fire crackling, the primus hissing and the water plop-plopping on the tarpaulin sheet passes between them.

"How do you feel?"

Josie raises a tear-streaked face to his and says almost to herself:

"Free. I feel free. How cool is that?"

The doctor rests his hands on Josie's shoulders and leads her to the window. His eyes scan hers.

"Good," he says. "Then we should make a move while the weather is fine. But we need to take care. The mountains will be treacherous with ice."

He steps away from her, pulls a packet from his rucksack and places it next to the beakers.

"Biscuit?"

He pours half-boiled water into his beaker and stirs it. His eyes follow the whirl of the liquid for a while and then, with a decisive movement, he puts the beaker on the table.

"OK - on the way down, I shall tell you my story. You will see that it belongs with yours. But I must warn you; I can only tell this on the run and over my shoulder, you understand?"

Twenty minutes later, our belongings are in the rucksacks on our backs, and we are in the open air. Pulling at the door, I remind myself that, on entering the hut yesterday evening, I was half-expecting to see the spirit of my father, his blond lover and the evil Christian Von Stoutenberg. But just a few hours later, it is the hut with no name and the other products of my childhood imagination on which I now close the door. It is high time I turned my back on these fantasies and walked away.

Shoulder to shoulder, the doctor and Josie are irregular outlines in the mist and some way in front of me. As soon as we hit the ridge, we are sliding, and our feet carve furrows in the mud and the snow. Josie seems none the worse for her fall and is steady on her feet. Nonetheless, every now and then, she rubs at her eyes and fingers her forehead. My guess is that she is suffering from double-vision and headaches, and we make slow progress towards the nick in the ridge.

The doctor is putting himself at a distance from us. I cannot say at what point he decides to begin his story, but his voice announces his presence long before I see him.

"My father was a very keen mountaineer, you know. He often used the hut as a base for his expeditions."

Disconcerted by the voice, I slip on the snow and land with a bump, my feet flying in the air. The doctor pays no attention to my clumsiness. He is waiting until Josie is by his side.

"What happened here in 1939 I know only from second-hand sources. I was barely 12 months old when my father was shot dead."

There is no time for comment. He is off again. His rucksack is large but tight to his back and he impresses me with his vitality. Leaning forward on bent knees, he is aggressively leading with his heels and plunging them into the snow. He slows to a walk and is muttering under his breath when we catch up with him.

"I was twelve when I discovered that my father was a murderer in his own right."

I barely acknowledge the doctor's statement. I am finding the snow tiresome and the mist irritating. It soaks my hair, and drops of moisture roll down the back of my neck.

"In 1939, he arrived in *Oberwald* with orders to clean up the town and Germanise it. It is ironic that he was actually born in *Bolzano* when it was still part of Austria. They say that when *Bolzano* became Italian in 1918, he refused to accept Mussolini's Italianisation programme and he became known as "The German." He was still a young boy at that time, but the nickname was a source of pride to him and he came to see himself as the most German of Germans. They also say that when he first arrived in *Oberwald*, he terrified people by his mere presence. He was a giant of a man, dominating everyone with an overwhelming sense of his own power and authority."

He wipes his nose with the cuff of his jacket, turns again and scoots into the mist. He shouts over his shoulder:

"They even say he ordered the killing of the people commemorated on the *Kreuzberg* monument."

We clamber after him until we reach the end of the ridge. From there, the path descends safely into the valley. The cloud is thinning and the earth below is visible yet unfamiliar. Rolling up and down the mountain, the cloud seems to be steaming from the earth.

"You know," the doctor says, "the army has always denied involvement in the killings. I have even heard it said that the villagers were responsible. But I guess memorials create their own truths. My father's name is forever damned. Who knows what really happened?"

Josie raises her arms and holds the palms of her hands towards the sky.

"Does it, like, matter now?"

I roll my eyes upwards in a bid to look thoughtful but the doctor roars his disagreement into Josie's face.

"Matter? Of course, it matters."

She shudders at the force of these words, screws up

her eyes and grimaces as if suffering sharp pain. But she remains otherwise unruffled by the doctor's pent-up frustration and anger. She whispers:

"So – what are you doing about it?"

A moment of stillness follows while the doctor expresses an apology with his face.

"You have to look at the facts and deal with them," he says. "Confronting the past is essential for forgiveness. You must do this in a world in which the people around you sweep the past under the carpet and pretend it never happened."

The doctor is upset and seems in danger of getting angry again. He is clenching and unclenching his hands, and there is little trace of the confident professional man I met yesterday. But Josie lowers her head and squints into his face.

"Tell us, yeah? What are these facts that you have to deal with?"

"My father helped send thousands of Jews to the camps before he came to *Oberwald*."

The words are hardly out of his mouth when I see a mixture of fear and confusion register in his eyes. He straightens his rucksack, hurtles over the rocks and plunges towards the village. It is all we can do to keep up with him, but Josie is persistent. She calls out:

"How did you find out?"

He stops unexpectedly, and Josie and I have to swerve to avoid bumping into him. The doctor steps backwards and looks Josie in the eye.

"I grew up with a lot of unspoken secrets," he says. "My family resisted my efforts to poke around in the past. Despite this resistance, I spent lonely hours in libraries and, later, on the internet researching into my father. When he was appointed SS leader of this region, his reputation as a ruthlessly efficient man preceded him. Had he lived, he would have rounded up the Jews in

*Oberwald* and sent them to the camps. Of this, there is no doubt."

He raises his eyebrows and smiles faintly.

"I felt numb after I read about what he did. For many years I was ashamed to tell anybody about him, but then I realized that my own silence was eating me up from inside."

Josie's eyes are concentrated and fearless.

"So, you unburdened yourself, yeah?"

The doctor nods.

"In the beginning, strangers looked at me with distrust when I told them about my father. It was as if I had inherited his personality. I was guilty, even though I hadn't committed a crime myself."

He turns his back on Josie and me and heads towards the distant sounds of life that reach out to us from the valley. Shapes emerge from far away and occasional lights flicker in *Oberwald*. We follow the doctor out of the mist and down towards the forest. We now have our backs to the world of black and white and we face one of faded colour that stands out against a thin layer of snow. We eventually come to a halt by the side of the stream. The doctor says:

"Every year I come here to the place where he died. I remember in gratitude the father who gave me life and I try to forgive and honour him."

I remain still and listen to my own heartbeat. I dare not speak for fear of asking the question his silence demands. It is Josie, as usual, who puts my question into her own words:

"And have you?"

For a moment we stand still, and not a word passes amongst the three of us. The only sound is that of the stream rushing downwards towards *Oberwald*.

"You've forgiven him, yeah?"

The doctor holds out his arm, the palm of his hand

facing outwards as if he would push away the edge of irritation that has crept into Josie's voice.

"It's not so simple. It depends on which man you are talking about. There is the father to whom I owe my existence – a father I love to this day. Then there is the father who committed terrible crimes. I have to make this distinction. My father and my father's deeds are two different things."

Nearby, a thin line of black catches my eye. The snow lies ruffled on the ground and is a reminder that we passed this place yesterday. Now, I am seeing it for the first time. With this renewal of vision comes the unexpected arrival of a desire to contact Liz and Marie-Claude. I acknowledge its presence and shelve it while the doctor continues with his story.

"I cannot allow him, someone I never knew, to dictate to me from the grave. I think I have made my own life. But even this I question. The past stamps us in ways that are often unknown to us. Did I become a person who saves life because my father took life?"

The doctor's question passes through my head like the memory of a dream. An urgent need has replaced my initial and simple desire, and what I have to say to Liz and Marie-Claude will not wait.

*Dear Marie-Claude, of course I shall see you in Brighton.*

*Liz, we need to discuss our future. We've been married for 7 years...*

"Has your father dictated to you?" the doctor said. "There is always time for change. You can always make up your own endings. Unless you do that, you can predict your own futures as surely as you can predict where those footprints end up."

The doctor appears to turn his thoughts inwards but Josie is not finished with him yet.

"This man who killed your father, yeah? Have you

215

kind of forgiven him?"

"Who is to forgive?" the doctor says. "It is true that the more I researched the life of my father, the more I got interested in his death. Who shot him and why? Finding answers to these questions was not easy. Many documents were destroyed in 1945, but the task was not impossible."

"Cool. Where did you start?"

"I researched the victims memorialised on the *Kreuzberg*."

"Yeah, and?"

"Only Miriam Dornacher was from *Oberwald*. She also had an older brother. When I first came here in 1965, there were still many people around who had known them both."

"How cool is that, and what did they say?"

"Brother and sister adored each other, apparently," the doctor said. "The people said that Miriam was a real fire-eater, a doer who refused to be the victim. Her brother Nicholas was quiet and shy - a jeweller by trade."

"And?"

"And do you know what they remembered about him?"

The doctor looks from Josie to me and then shifts his gaze to look past us both. There is the barest outline of a smile on his face when he says:

"They told me he was very vain and very short-sighted. They said that outside his shop, he refused to wear his glasses for fear of ridicule."

The doctor lets his eyes flicker sideways and with a finality that suggests he wants to conclude his story, he adds:

"Imagine that. The whole of a man's life condensed into a couple of phrases."

Josie steps forward and seeks out the doctor's eyes

with hers.

"And did they tell you what happened to him?"

"Nobody knew. They said that Nicholas disappeared along with most *Oberwalder* Jews soon after my father's death. My research found him in New York from 1947 until his death there in 1991. A successful man, he set up the New York jeweller's guild and was its president until his death. I often wondered if he killed my father."

Josie looks at him in a way that suggests she has seen some terrible vision. Then, her gaze appears to turn towards the birth of a thought inside her head. Her eyes rotate lazily, following the thought while it settles in her consciousness.

"He didn't kill him though, did he?"

The question tag has a downward tone that suggests Josie has not asked a question. It is confirmation she is asking for. The doctor is non-committal.

"Oh, it's possible. He had a motive. Maybe, he believed, as many people did then, that my father ordered the killing of the Jews and was therefore responsible for murdering his sister. Acts of revenge are quite common. He might also have believed that by killing my father he was preventing the deaths of other *Oberwalder* Jews."

I wag my head in an attempt to throw out the notion that is developing there. Josie continues to look at him with unblinking eyes in the manner of one who has received a revelation.

"That didn't happen though, did it?"

The doctor spreads his hands wide.

"Who can say? It is true that at around that time, most *Oberwald* Jews found their way out of Germany to safety." The doctor looks down at his hands and gently rubs them together. Then he holds them still, his palms together as if in prayer.

"Perhaps my father's death gave them the time they

needed to get out."

He swings round and sets off again. Following on behind, I have the pleasant sensation that every step is taking me further from my old self and further from my old life. I wonder if I will ever be able to find my back to the way it was. I feel the words of a question forming, feel them poised on my lips but it is Josie, always a step ahead of me, who finds the courage to ask the question that hovers on my lips.

"So, Nicholas pulled the trigger, yeah?"

The doctor responds with a shrug. I cannot say whether this is an expression of indifference or of ignorance. Nor can I say whether the lift of his eyebrows indicates surprise or uncertainty.

"If he was as short-sighted as they say," he says, "he couldn't have killed anyone with such a clean shot; unless, of course, he was extraordinarily lucky."

For a moment, Josie's face remains still, but in reaction to some imagined danger, her eyes are suddenly sharp and focused.

"It had to be an accomplice, yeah?"

"Good girl," the doctor says. "The crack on your head has helped you see the light. Whoever the accomplice was, he must have been a – how do you English say – a crack shot."

I spin round in the manner of a person who refuses to see something unacceptable. The words, "crack" and "shot," set up a series of associations that confront me with a vague memory and then connect me to some words in my father's obituary. I sideline the connection and focus instead on Liz and Marie-Claude. How can I best put my thoughts into words?

*Dear Marie-Claude, I need to tell you something about Liz and I.*

*Liz, it's time we looked at our relationship and...*

The doctor is right in front of me and looking into my

eyes.

"Yes," he says. "I told you, did I not, that your story and mine are the same. They belong together."

"You know who this accomplice was, yeah?"

The doctor lets out a long sigh.

"Of course, I know. And you know, too," he says. "But my research came to an end there. My part is to forgive. Badness has to stop somewhere, don't you think? And it was fear of this badness that kept you awake, my friend, am I right? I was listening to you."

There is a heaving sound from behind. Josie is bent double, with her hands on her knees. The doctor rushes over and puts his arm around her shoulders.

"It's quite normal," he says. "Such a blow can make you throw up."

I do not know she has been sick until I see the mess at her feet and catch a whiff of digesting biscuits. There is no time to respond or reflect. Josie and I have to shuffle backwards to avoid the doctor's rucksack. He has swung round and is hurrying away into the heart of the forest.

"Take good care of her," he says over his shoulder and leaves us rooted to the spot.

A terrible tiredness comes over me, and the forest and the mountains are suddenly threatening places. I need to rush after him and to race down to the hotel and deal with Liz and Marie-Claude. Josie's voice reminds me I have someone else to take care of.

"Now we know, yeah? The agent was right, after all. It's all in his books."

"Especially *The White Mountain*."

"He might have called it *The Gay Assassin*."

These words bring with them a residue of resentment but I sweep this aside.

"He was just a human being,"

"The world changes when we do, yeah?"

219

I grab Josie by the arm, and with great care, I propel her down the mountain.

The church clock is striking 11 when the two of us emerge from the trees and walk along the *Kreuzberg* road. We enter the central square to the sound of our own footsteps. Windows blaze with light and, from the houses, the cosy sounds of cutlery clanging and bottles clinking emerge and there is an odour of sausages and bread in the air. The rain begins to fall lightly as we turn our backs on the square and arrive at our hotel. At the push of my hand the glass door swings back.

I hover in the lobby; anxious to go up to my room. But we cannot avoid the hotel manager. He goes through the motions of being pleased to see us.

"Your friend has arranged everything," he says. "The town doctor is on his way now."

He leads Josie away to a corner table, and waiters appear at the flick of his fingers. Left alone, I dash up the stairs to settle my future. Ten minutes later, I am back in the lobby. The young town doctor has arrived. His windcheater is hanging over the arm of a chair and he is listening to Dr Hackfeld and holding a small flashlight at Josie's ear. Dr Hackfeld has his rucksack is on his back, and he is half-turned towards the door.

"I want to thank you," I say.

"She'll be fine in a day or two."

"Is it over," I ask.

"It's over," he says.

"I'd say it was only just beginning," says a voice.

Stefan is standing beside us.

"Look what they have done to me."

He is wearing sunglasses but his eyes are swollen and his bottom lip is cut. He points to his face.

"I should have learned from history," he says. "You don't mess with the people of *Oberwald*. I think they were trying to tell me something. Cover up is not the most popular topic for a newspaper article in this town. No, it isn't over yet."

Behind me, I hear the glass door closing. Turning, I see the doctor in the street. He looks me right in the eyes and raises an arm. He is holding his hand palm outwards, fingers fluttering like a butterfly's wings. It might be a gesture of farewell. To me it looks like he is allowing the remnants of distant time to slip through his fingers. He feels it for a moment and then discards it to the wind.

# 16

A year has passed since my father's funeral, and Liz and I are now standing before another celebrant and in another church. This is a service for which lateness was not an option. We are its focus and its mainstay. Without us, there will be no event.

"A wedding is a celebration of falling in love and beginning a marriage," the celebrant says. "A renewal of vows is a celebration of staying in love and staying married."

I cannot say that the idea to renew our vows was one I reflected on. The decision was there in my head while the doctor, Josie and I made our way down from the mountain hut. I rang Liz from my hotel room in *Oberwald* and, immediately after, I emailed Marie-Claude and told her. Nonetheless, I did go to the summer school at the end of August last year. Avoiding Marie-Claude would have given her a power over my actions I did not want her to have.

"As Nicholas and Liz have already found, in every marriage more than a week old, there are grounds for divorce. What they've found is their own ground for marriage."

I silently offer up thanks. I have at last thrown off the need to compare everyone with the perfect father who never was. I am now able to list my own grounds for marriage. At the top of that list is that I married a human being.

"And just as we celebrate our successes - whatever they might be - so today, Nicholas and Liz are celebrating their achievement in being successful at marriage."

Selected members of family and friends are here. I picked up my mother, and she is sitting next to Robby. Ben is more interested in his new toy.

"Today, on this, their wedding anniversary, Nicholas and Liz take the opportunity, to rededicate themselves to each other, celebrating what they've accomplished and looking ahead to what they still want to do with their lives."

Josie is here and looking radiant with her new man. They are now engaged, and she says she is looking forward to starting a family. I am very pleased that both Miriam and Petra sent cards of congratulations. They wished us well and expressed their happiness that at least Josie would be there to represent their side of the family. I have heard nothing from Tony. I assume he is still expecting me to run off with the family silver.

"They have invited you, their relatives and friends, to share with them this celebration. Many of you of you were present 7 years ago when Nicholas and Liz exchanged their wedding vows."

I am now about to make my pledge, but I can't stop reflecting on the happiness and sadness Robby evokes in me. When he arrived earlier, I noticed that he was alone. Later, he confirmed what I had already guessed - he and his wife are now separated. Before I could offer any words of advice or wisdom he said:

"Dad, don't look so surprised." He then gave me that confrontational stare of his and added: "And don't even think of giving me any advice. You know it and I know it – that divorce runs in the family."

"And before Liz and Nicholas make their pledges, Nicholas has asked me to read a verse from the Persian poet Omar Khayyam."

He reaches into the folds of his cassock and pulls out a worn old postcard with a photograph of the *Kreuzberg* on it. He says:

"Don't seek to recall yesterday that is past, Nor repine for tomorrow which has yet to come; Don't build your hopes on the past or the future, Be happy now and don't live on wind."

At that point, a ray of sunlight bursts through the church window and breaks over me. My father was not present at our wedding ceremony in 2003. He is here now though and firmly connected to me in the way he promised when I was a child. He is present in my shadow, now spreading across the aisle and over the pews. What the shadow holds is not the perfect person of my dreams. This is simply Charles Saddler, the man. Charles Saddler – my father.